THE LEGACY SERIES

SERIES TITLES

The Machine We Trust
Tim Conrad

Gridlock
Brett Biebel

Salt Folk
Ryan Habermeyer

The Commission of Inquiry
Patrick Nevins

Maximum Speed
Kevin Clouther

Reach Her in This Light
Jane Curtis

The Spirit in My Shoes
John Michael Cummings

*The Effects of Urban Renewal on Mid-Century America and
Other Crime Stories*
Jeff Esterholm

What Makes You Think You're Supposed to Feel Better
Jody Hobbs Hesler

Fugitive Daydreams
Leah McCormack

Hoist House: A Novella & Stories
Jenny Robertson

Finding the Bones: Stories & A Novella
Nikki Kallio

ing of 4-H club, vacation bible school and The Hunger Games? You couldn't, because I guarantee you'd be sent home within the week for losing your flock to wolves, or speeding interstate semis. The only way you'll ever make it to the final show and the crowning of 'Shepherd of the Summer' is through these pages. So nestle in—just as if you were curling up in Paul Bunyan's enormous outstretched palm—and enjoy the wonder of stories only Tim Conrad could bring you. I just adore this book!"

—Thisbe Nissen
author of *How Other People Make Love*

"Tim Conrad's debut story collection takes readers through an American Midwest filled with men and women living on the margins, surrounded by chain-link fences, both resented and needed, not just of the landscape but of the heart. The characters striving in this forgotten America are smart and kind and lost, disappointed by the men in their lives, yet determined to carve out a place in this world. Together, these stories are a tender portrait of our desire for love and acceptance, all told in language that is suspenseful, moving, and perfectly written."

—Michael Nye
author of *Until We Have Faces*

THE MACHINE WE TRUST

STORIES

TIM CONRAD

CORNERSTONE PRESS
UNIVERSITY OF WISCONSIN-STEVENS POINT

Cornerstone Press, Stevens Point, Wisconsin 54481
Copyright © 2024 Tim Conrad
www.uwsp.edu/cornerstone

Printed in the United States of America by
Point Print and Design Studio, Stevens Point, Wisconsin

Library of Congress Control Number: 2024930285
ISBN: 978-1-960329-20-2

Cornerstone Press titles are produced in courses and internships offered by the Department of English at the University of Wisconsin–Stevens Point.

DIRECTOR & PUBLISHER
Dr. Ross K. Tangedal

EXECUTIVE EDITORS
Jeff Snowbarger, Freesia McKee

EDITORIAL DIRECTOR
Ellie Atkinson

SENIOR EDITORS
Brett Hill, Grace Dahl

PRESS STAFF
Madalyn Carpenter, Carolyn Czerwinski, Alex Diaz, Sophie McPherson, Kylie Newton, Eva Nielsen, Josh Paulson, Natalie Reiter, Lauren Rudesill, Katie Schimke, Ava Willett

To K.N.—for believing

STORIES

"Attention is love. I believe that."

—Lynne Barrett, *Magpies*

DUTCH TREAT

Technically, I was homeschooled, but we never really had a home. My mother was a writer and professor who had made a career out of her skepticism toward traditional education.

That winter we moved back to Nebraska for our second stint there. Upon reentering the Midwest, my mother said, "It takes a sturdy people to hold up a sky this big," an aphorism she'd offered before and was fond of repeating. The signs along the interstate proclaimed Nebraska the home of Arbor Day. "It's probably because they have so few trees. Where there's a dearth, there's love."

As always, she could have been talking about anything.

My mother had written a couple books about experiential learning, and, having done so, was in demand among a certain sect of liberal arts colleges. Experiential learning was just then coming into vogue, and the schools wanted someone to come and help their students round out their expensive educations with real world experience. Mother obliged. She would arrive and teach her mutant version of service learning for a semester, in which she placed honors students as intern garbage collectors and strip club bouncers. It was pioneering work. The students would read her first book, *Writing in the Margins*, then cheerfully head off to night jobs as janitors and liquor store clerks.

The colleges, I suppose, loved it. It was first-hand experience in seldom-championed society, and the students kept in touch with my mother for years, writing emails to her about how their experiences had moved them in profound ways, about how they now better understood their father/sister/ex-boyfriend/neighborhood bum. One of her most gifted students—a boy she'd given a fake ID and placed as a blackjack dealer—wrote frequently. He kept her abreast of the fulfilling work he'd eventually found as an accountant and urged us to drop by his workplace, a riverboat casino in Rising Sun, Indiana.

Sometimes, she made me take jobs—menial jobs that were part of my maturation and self-actualization. Mostly, I think my mother was worried I wasn't getting enough social interaction. I never had residency in the states we lived in, and for years, I wasn't able to work legally, so most of my work was done off the record. Once, in Maryland, my mother sent me out with blue crab fisherman for three weeks and gave me a list of discussion questions we were to address upon my return. Among them: *3) Compare and Contrast the gender identity of the men you met with the portrayal of masculinity found in Melville, or alternatively, London. And: 8) How did your experience alter or reinforce your ideas about the commercial seafood industry?*

In addition to the part-time jobs, I read incessantly and sat in on classes at the universities where she taught. I tried to make a list of everything the campuses had in common with one another: *squirrels, deciduous trees, Toyota Priuses. At least one architectural monstrosity. Lots of white people.* At sixteen, I had already internalized the word *ubiquitous.* The students were seldom seen except in migration to and from classes and on unseasonably warm days when they littered the green spaces in improbable admission-brochure clusters.

Sometimes, I loitered close enough to conversations to work on my slang. Mostly, everyone ignored me.

I know it sounds a bit solitary, but it was a good life. I lacked for little, and my mother was proud of me. If nothing else, my ability to articulate my thoughts and interact with others was proof her system worked. And sometimes, she needed this reassurance.

* * *

Upon arrival in Nebraska, we moved in across town from the college, far from where students lived in bland apartment complexes and shabby, subdivided houses. My mother encouraged me to wander around in those areas though if I felt compelled. "The kegs are usually outside, so parties are easy to crash," she said. "Help yourself. Just avoid the ones where there's chanting and don't carry anything valuable."

We settled into a cheap modular in a subdivision named Dutch Treat; its entrance sign loomed like cruel joke beside a miniature windmill. The house had a wooden fence but no driveway. The street had no curbs, and the grass on either side was rutted from the daily ad lib parking of its residents. Just before the railroad tracks, the street bent sideways and ran alongside them, nothing but a chain link fence to separate the neighborhood from the noise.

Inside the house, the carpet smelled of cats and smoke. The college had offered to provide something more becoming of my mother's prestigious visiting professorship, but she declined it. "I need to live what I teach," I heard her say over the phone.

To me, she said, "No jokes."

We knew we wouldn't be there long. My mother and I never stayed anywhere more than eight months. She said, "If you stay somewhere long enough to add to its population, you've stayed too long." On where I was born, in San Antonio, she said, "It was happenstance. I wanted to go abroad and give you dual citizenship, but the closest I came was Texas."

My father was an idiot savant of some kind. I never knew him. My mother said it wasn't necessary that he be part of my life, that she'd wanted a child and had chosen my father not out of love, but out of desire for me. She made it sound like a sort of romance between us. She said that if I wanted to meet him someday, she'd finance it and even tell me where to find him, but that I wasn't ready for it yet. "I nearly went to a sperm bank," she said, "but that seemed excessive." She was frank about such things.

Once, on the way across Iowa, she told me about reproduction, and we stopped at a video store that had viewing rooms in the back. She talked to the manager—I have no idea what she said or did to convince him—selected a video and fed quarters to the machine as she narrated. "It's not all like this," she said, "but it's best if you know this now, if you see it with your mother in the room."

At various times, she encouraged me to sleep around. At others, she told me to "strongly consider" that I might be gay. Whenever a hosting professor had children my age— regardless of gender—she'd subtly try to set me up with them. "That's the one part of your education I can't help you with," she'd say. "At least not with the actual experiments."

My mother slept with a great many men. I knew this at the time. They were a constant presence in our travels, like stagehands who lingered just beyond the lights and who rushed onto the stage, when invited, to change the scenery.

*　*　*

What I chiefly remember about those years is the car rides. My mother didn't believe in airplane travel. She said it was dishonest, that it misrepresented the scale of the world. The only time we did fly, she wouldn't let me sleep during the flight. She said, "It's not natural to take a nap that starts in Fort Worth and ends in St. Louis." She also said, "Stewardesses are descended from magician's assistants. They maintain the façade of the act and misdirect your attention from how terribly wrong things might go. That's why they dress like that and stand at the entrances, why they do everything with such flourish." But by the attention she paid them, I could tell she admired them.

My mother was full of such theories and contradictions. She listened to the radio on car rides, because to her it was a form of optimism. She listened despite her belief that disc jockeys were some of the least-evolved humans. She never ate at chain restaurants, but she admitted there was something reassuring in their ubiquity. She believed there was nothing worse than not having opinions.

She was not superstitious.

And my mother was right in saying I wasn't ready to meet my father. He was far from my mind. The largest role he had in any of my daydreams: I imagined someday the absence of a father figure might provide common ground in meeting someone special. At my jobs, I was constantly running into people who hadn't known their fathers. I never prompted it. Once, when I was a brick mason, the crew somehow stumbled onto the topic at lunch. When I pressed the matter, two-thirds confessed they had no relationship with their biological fathers, but instead of feeling a connection, it made me feel inexplicably lonely. I withdrew from the conversation and went to mix mortar and mull over one of my mother's questions: *6) What connections might one make between contemporary house construction and the oft-referenced suburban angst?*

The jobs were a dizzying series of multi-week apprenticeships, usually complete with a father figure site mentor, who would show me the ropes and hover around my work just often enough to make sure I wasn't killing myself or creating more work for others. They all had short or thinning hair and monosyllabic names. "Will," I would ask, "am I holding this trowel right?" or "Wade, show me again how to tie this knot." I never asked them the questions on my sheets: *8) The real estate industry trains their agents to call houses homes. Does it represent a harmless semantic shift?* They just weren't that sort of audience.

* * *

Not long before arriving in Nebraska we'd adopted a dog, a lethargic mutt named Melba. I was under the suspicion pretty much from the get-go that having her was supposed to teach me something about parenting, and with it, knock down one of the few remaining barriers between my mother and myself. I predicted too that my mother probably wouldn't let me keep her for more than three or four states.

We'd picked Melba out of a no-kill shelter in Idaho. The fact that it was a no-kill shelter was very important to my mother. "You never want to start your relationship with another creature by believing you're saving its life."

That much was true, especially since I believed what I did about her impending abandonment.

During the early weeks at Dutch Treat, I mostly sat in front of a ceramic space heater and read *My Ántonia*, which had been assigned by my mother. She was in the process of finding a placement for me, which is something that I could have done for myself if I'd ever had residency. In one of the great mysteries of those years, she somehow maintained an Illinois driver's license even though we only lived there once and only for four weeks.

Had I not been reading Cather, I might not have noticed the trailer arriving in the "mobile lifestyle community" a few blocks away. Or rather, I might have seen it, but I would not have taken much stock of the family that stood outside, watching the truck slot the trailer among the rest. There was a girl, about my age, with her arm in a cast and a ponytail draped over her shoulder. A pair of heavyset adults flanked her: a man in a ballcap and a woman in an ill-fitting shirt. I came to a stop and watched the truck inch backward. Every so often the man driving would hop down and check on the precise alignment; he didn't seem to trust the family's help. As I loitered, Melba began taking an interest in what was going on. Eventually, she caught wind of something on the ground and began pulling me in their direction.

"Whoa, girl," I said. "What are you after?"

I'd been reading a lot of Westerns. I pulled at the leash but felt cruel redirecting her too forcefully. I let her pull me closer to the truck. The driver was down from his perch again, the truck's air brakes hissing over a diesel throbbing.

Melba must have lost whatever scent she'd been chasing. She let up on the leash and waddled over to a set of mailboxes to pee. I watched her, and when I looked up again, the girl from the family was standing very close, much closer than I would have thought possible, given the timing.

"Name?" she asked. She held out her hand for Melba, fingers together, just like the man at the no-kill shelter had taught me to do.

I almost said my own. "Melba," I said. "Yours?"

"Nikki," she said. "We're going to get a dog this week. A puppy."

"What kind?" I asked, not knowing what else to say.

"A free one."

She laughed before it occurred to me she was making a joke. From over her shoulder, the man called her name, and just as easily as she had appeared, she receded.

* * *

The semester itself passed quickly. I was bored but not unaccustomed to being so. My mother found a placement for me at a local convenience store working the graveyard shift. She told me it was all that was available. "Since you've already worked in meatpacking, that is," she said, and I nodded.

"I don't want to be a meatpacker again," I said.

"No, I didn't think so."

So, I started working at the gas station. It sold Conoco Phillips gas. The owner was foreign and contemptuous of the town. The whole county was dry, so there wasn't much business after midnight. Many of the customers bought only gas and paid at the pump. Others came in for cigarettes and fountain drinks. I sat behind my bulletproof glass and watched the world spin, occasionally overriding the prepay mandate on a pump for a respectable-looking cash customer. On my sheet, my mother had given me the question: *2) In what ways does modern business still operate on white privilege and affluent right-of-way?* I imagined this meant I was supposed to turn on the pumps for minority customers, and so I did. A lot of people who came in complained about gas prices, but the only people who ever did drive-offs were white.

Also on the sheet: *8) To what is sitting behind bulletproof glass analogous?* I kept the questions in my back pocket. I spent most of my time stocking displays and wondering how my mother found such jobs. I was envious of her students this semester, the ones she'd placed as farm laborers and housekeepers.

* * *

One day, near the end of term, I had Melba out in the backyard. Through the gating in the back, I saw a rogue puppy in the alley. Melba seemed curious, so I opened the gate and let in the stray. Melba circled and sniffed it.

The gate swung open. Nikki stood just beyond the threshold, leash in hand. "What are you doing?" she asked.

"My dog was lonely," I said.

I wasn't sure she remembered me, but she said hello to Melba as though they saw each other every other morning. To me, she said, "You never told me your name."

I told her.

"Why don't I see you at school?"

"I'm homeschooled."

It seemed like she was waiting for more, but I really didn't want to go into it. "You don't seem like it," she said. She told me that she was a junior at the local high school and that it was just as well that I was homeschooled, because it sucked there.

Our dogs were getting along well. Beyond introductions, I didn't know what else to say, so I asked if she liked ice cream. She said she couldn't have dairy, and just as smoothly as she'd come, she gathered the puppy and went back out the gate. It was as if she'd dematerialized. I briefly wondered if I was the only one who could see her.

But she came back again the next day, opened the gate, and gave me a popsicle. It was mid-April and unseasonably hot, so I welcomed it. When I took it, I felt how warm her hand was.

She came by a few times after that, always barefoot. We didn't have much to say.

Instead, we sat and ate the things I found for us in our kitchen refrigerator—cold pieces of ham, leftover Chinese, and miscellaneous vegetables. Nikki took my offerings silently, as though she'd already resigned herself to whatever meager things I might provide.

* * *

One night around that time, my mother came home and got to ranting about her students' progress. I suppose she intended it to be inspirational, but often she lapsed into airing her frustrations. She told me about the semester's prison guard, and about her bread truck drivers.

The latter was, in her words, "a marvel." She told me that together, four students completed one route four days a week. They intercepted each other and switched off in parking lots. "The communal aspect is simply a bonus," she said. "And I have a female plumber," she added. "Her resolve is commendable, but she's still not beyond stereotypes. I'll spare you her jokes."

I nodded. I pictured Nikki as a plumber and began making my mother a second margarita. I was often her bartender, a role I'd enjoyed since I turned twelve. But my mother wasn't an alcoholic.

"They're all just so unimaginative this semester. And I have this other student," she continued, "that's working at a pig farm. He told me today that in his final paper, he plans to compare himself to the prodigal son."

"Is it an organic farm?" I asked.

She laughed and lit a cigarette. "You know, men used to think women like me were prostitutes," she said and laughed again.

"I'm still working through Loren Eiseley," I said because I didn't know what else to say. "When do we need to discuss it?"

"You have as long as you need to understand things. You know that." She looked at me expectantly, and I nearly told her about Nikki. My mother was fond of using silence as a weapon and had told me so on several occasions. It seemed like somehow she already knew, but I felt the need to protect Nikki.

"Sometimes," she said, "my students confuse having secrets with maturity." She took a sip of her drink and looked up at the clock. She wouldn't look me in the eye. She believed that, in tense situations, eye contact was animalistic and challenging. "Want to see a movie tonight before work?"

I said that I did.

*　*　*

The next week was the last one in the term. My mother's students were busy with their final portfolios, and I was scrambling to finish my required reading. I seldom took out Melba, and when I did, I didn't see Nikki.

But on Thursday—sometime after midnight—Nikki walked up to my window at the gas station. She had on shoes and a loose white sweatshirt over faded jeans. She'd been crying. My mother always said people cried because they couldn't master their emotions. I tried not to think of this.

She didn't bother with small talk. "Can I come in?" she asked.

I went to the front doors and slid the slid the deadbolt out of the way. I tried to be smooth about it by looking at her and not at the key, but I failed. I pulled on the door and it rattled against its pins.

When I finally got it open, she said, "Is there any chance I can sleep in here tonight?"

I was scheduled to work until 7 a.m. I said it'd be fine but that she'd have to be out by the time I opened the doors at 6 a.m.

She nodded. "I probably won't stay that long," she said. "I just need to sleep for an hour or so."

I knew Mr. Singh only had two security cameras, one on the front door and one on the registers, so I led her inside and picked out a spot in front of the back wall of coolers, where the cooling apparatus blew out warm exhaust. I went to the back and broke down some cardboard boxes and laid them on the tiles. I gave her my sweatshirt, even though she had one and, for good measure, an undersized travel blanket from one of the front displays.

She thanked me and fell asleep in minutes.

With her there, the store seemed even quieter. I had turned off the music earlier and could now hear the whir of the frozen Coke machine across the room. During her nap, only a few customers came by, one of which bought cigarettes at the window. I briefly entertained the notion that she was hiding from someone and that the person might need gas as they were driving around looking for her, but even I knew that was ridiculous.

When she woke up, she was hungry, and I offered her a seat behind the counter. It was the only one there. The owner wanted to discourage loitering. She accepted. I went into the aisles and grabbed a bag of Funyuns and a cream soda. "Do you like these?" I asked. My mother believed that anything with *fun* in the name was worthy of sympathy.

"Sure," she said and smiled. She held up my book, a used copy of *My Ántonia*. "Are you reading this?" she asked. When I nodded, she told me everyone at her school had to read it in tenth grade. "I mean," she said, reaching for our cream soda, "it's pretty bad, right? And our English teacher said that Jim's gay."

I'd been reading the book but hadn't picked up on this. "Why's he say that? Because Cather is gay?"

"Who?"

"Willa Cather. The author."

"Oh," she said. She held a Funyun up in the air. "That totally makes sense!"

That hadn't been my point, but I let it go.

We talked most of the night. No customers came. She told me about her family, about how she didn't know her mom, that the woman I'd seen moving in with them was Rose, a woman she didn't know what to call. She told me she wanted to be a dancer but that she'd probably go to school for something more practical if she got the chance. She told me she hated ranch dressing even though her dad bought it by the gallon at Sam's Club.

When she was leaving, almost exactly at six, she suddenly remembered the travel blanket, which she'd worn on her lap most of the night, and offered it back to me, but I declined.

"Won't you get in trouble?" she asked.

Having a vagrant minor stay in the store for most of the night seemed a bigger problem, but I was touched by her concern. "It should be all right," I said. "My boss won't take inventory for another few weeks."

"Won't you get in trouble then?"

"Well, yes, I mean, I probably would," I said," but I'm moving in a week."

She nodded thoughtfully and took a step toward the automatic doors which, unlocked by some invisible timer, slid open for her.

"Then we don't have much time, do we?" she said and walked out.

* * *

The last evening we were in town, my mother was invited to eat dinner with several of the tenured professors—one of whom was interested in her romantically. She said he'd asked her out for drinks afterward. It was her third scholar of the semester. She was excited. "You can always depend on these people." She said she'd be home late.

"I won't be here," I reminded her.

"I know, but I thought you might be happy for me."

I said I was.

That night, Nikki came back. She was riding in a car full of kids. She came up to my window and said that they were going to a festival, and that there was room in the back seat.

I said, "I'm working."

She said, "You should close." She was wearing a tank top with thin straps. Just looking at her shoulders made me feel cold, even though it was impossible to tell the temperature through the thick glass.

"Okay. Give me a minute." I didn't have a closing procedure; the store was always open. I wished I had a better reason for leaving than I did, so I left the owner a note: *Sorry about closing. Possible food poisoning?* Had I given it more time, I probably could have come up with something better, but at least I kept it brief. Mom always said you can spot liars because they're the ones who say too much.

I found a key beneath the counter and locked up. The backseat was crowded. She introduced me to her friends, we hopped in, and the driver peeled out. Nikki sat half on the seat and half on my lap. The road was straight and the driver drove with his knees. Nikki's hair blew in my face. And suddenly all I could smell was coconuts.

I hadn't considered it, but I should have realized the festival would be closed when we got there. It was around 3 a.m. and dark, but as drove in, we could see a Ferris wheel towering over everything else. The festival was set up right on Main Street. We parked a couple of blocks away and began walking. The others were drunk, but I couldn't smell anything on Nikki. I tried.

Reaching the perimeter, we hopped a metal fence and began weaving through the tents. I realized now we were evenly matched—three boys and three girls—and we began to split off this way. Nikki and I headed for the wheel. My courage was disintegrating, and I grew nervous. My mother said that if you act boldly, no one will have the strength of character to condemn you. I thought of this, but acting bold seemed useless in the dark. I felt my body betraying me. Nikki took my hand. I was shaking.

She said, "Isn't this great?"

I said it was.

"My dad never used to take me to fairs," she said. "He thought they were full of tricksters."

"Tricksters?" I asked, interested. I'd read the *Odyssey*. My mother had taught me they were heroic.

"Well, that's my word. He called them something worse."

We reached the Ferris wheel and hopped the gate. I helped her over and ended up with my arm around her. It felt surprisingly natural, as though the night had been conspiring for such a moment. We climbed up to the platform. One of the baskets was waiting for us, the bar raised in salute, but Nikki didn't want that one. She grabbed onto the edge of the wheel and started climbing. I watched; her movements were fluid and spoke to a childhood spent scaling things.

"You coming?" she said.

I'd never done anything like it. The metal was painted silver and was cold to the touch. In the dark, it was hard to fully appreciate how high we were, but I took note as we drew even with and passed a set of second-story windows, and I felt the breeze hit us as we climbed above the building's roofline. I thought she was probably going for the top, but she found a basket on the front to the wheel that she liked and climbed in. She raised the bar for me, and only with her encouragement was I able to wrap myself around the front edge and heave myself into it.

She clicked our basket shut, which made me feel better.

Nikki said, "I can't believe we just did that. Don't you feel like Spiderman?"

"Sort of. I've never ridden one of these."

Nikki was out of breath. "I haven't either."

We sat in silence for a moment, recovering ourselves. I thought of what my mother had told me about nostalgia's ability to kill the present and how history shouldn't be the only thing people have in common.

"I'll bet it gets windy at the top," I said.

"Should we climb up there when we leave?"

"No, no," I said. I think I almost shouted it.

"I'll bet if you got on one big enough, you could see into the next county." I looked at her. I didn't know what to say to that, so I stayed silent.

After a pause, she turned to me. "What are you going to do with me," she said, in a whispery voice I wasn't expecting, "now that you have me up here."

I didn't know. I knew I was supposed to kiss her, so I did that. For a while it felt nice, albeit obligatory. Nikki climbed onto my lap crossways, put her bare arms around my neck, and tried to keep the kissing going, even though I jumped with each sway and jerk of the basket. She rammed her hand into the hair on the back of my head, and in spite of myself, I felt goosebumps all over my arms.

She stopped and sat up straight, holding my hands. "You can touch me wherever you like," she said.

Before I could consider this, we heard noises somewhere below, a clattering of metal on pavement. Then, the unmistakable sound of a bottle rocket being fired into the air. Nikki and I turned in our seat to watch. I didn't know whether her friends had found the fireworks in one of the tents or brought them along. Soon, there were louder sounds, firecrackers and cherry bombs. I myself wasn't unfamiliar with consumer-grade pyrotechnics, given all of our interstate travel.

Nikki laughed. "They're such idiots," she said, her sexy voice gone and her affection for them clear.

I couldn't have told you why, but her laughter punched me in the gut.

A light came on in one of the second-story windows, slightly below where we sat. The other kids scrambled around. One of them was carrying a bundle of lit sparklers, laughing like he'd discovered fire.

"Come on," Nikki said and tried to lift the bar on our basket. I reached over and tried to help, but even together—or perhaps because of our collective fumbling—we couldn't get it.

"I think we're stuck," I said and tried to laugh.

She plopped down, pressed her feet against the bar, and kicked until the metal gave. The bar came off in its entirety and rattled into the darkness below. Nikki laughed. "My dad says nothing happens without a little force."

At the window, a figure appeared and looked up at us. "Oh, for fuck's sake," he said. "You stupid kids trying to kill yourselves?"

* * *

When I finally got home, my mother was up and busy boxing up the living room. The semester had just ended, and we were headed for a summer residency in Wisconsin.

It wasn't time for me to be home from work. I hadn't thought to have them drop me off back at the store; there was a chance the owner wouldn't have noticed my absence without reviewing the security footage. The whole way back, the two boys up front had shot off bottle rockets and passed a fifth back and forth. When they offered it to me, I'd taken a few sips to be polite. I'd sat in the back with Nikki on my lap, trying not to notice how much the car was weaving.

"You smell like you've been at a White Snake show," my mother said when I came in the house. She wasn't upset. She looked me over as I sat down on the living room floor and began rubbing Melba's ears.

"Did you go slumming then?" my mother asked. It wasn't an accusation. She paused her packing and looked over at me. I stopped petting Melba, who looked at me as well.

I should have felt indignation, but instead, my chief concern was my innocence. "What are you talking about?"

My mother didn't answer right away. She resumed her packing, shoving her only shelf of books into an apple crate. "Did you learn my lesson?" she finally asked. I thought she had misspoke, but she hadn't. "It's not an easy one," she said. "There are things to be learned here."

I ignored her and started walking to my bedroom in the back of the house. I began packing. I didn't have much: a laptop, some clothes, and a few books—Mom believed in leaving good, completed books in public places as part of her pass-it-on system of learning. I thought I might be able to pack and leave before she reached me, but she came into my room as I was unplugging the computer.

"We don't need to do anything too formal, but I would like to discuss this," she said. "Knowing that you won't see her again, does this experience make you feel like an imperialist?"

"What?"

"It's common," she said. "It's what men do. I just want you to be aware of it."

I didn't know where to start. "Why are you obsessed with making me a man?"

"Who else is going to do it?" she asked. She tugged on a loose corner of a Bob Marley poster I'd recently picked up at a campus sale. "Why? Do you not want to be one?"

I didn't answer. I double-checked the closet and found a stray sock. I shoved it in my bag.

"I'm not sure I want to go with you to Indiana," I said. I knew as I said it that I was getting the state wrong but it hardly mattered. I half-wanted my mother to correct me.

"Did you have sex?" she said. "You can talk with me. It's all part of your education."

I grabbed my clothes and stormed out of the room. In the living room, I found Melba's leash, determined to take her with me, but when I got to the front door, she looked so sleepy I couldn't bring myself to drag her out into the dark. My mom only followed partway. Her voice was softer now. She said, "There will be others. What was her name?"

I knew she was changing her tack, trying to memorialize Nikki. I couldn't bear it. I pushed outside and slammed the door behind me. I imagined I only had a small head start. I imagined going back to the convenience store and returning the key to Mr. Singh. I imagined running for Nikki's trailer. In the car, she'd told me I could come over anytime, that her parents didn't care what she did, as long as she was quiet. She'd meant it suggestively, but it was the saddest thing anyone had ever said to me. I mostly remembered where she lived, and so I began to walk in that direction.

Above me, the sky was growing pale with morning, and as I entered the trailer park, I thought I would be able to find her place. Perhaps I was expecting flowers out front or some other sign of effort or beauty, but as I looked at the trailers in the low light of dawn, I felt ashamed that I could only see how similar they were, and I knew that I would never locate her.

Worse yet, even if I could, even if she took me in, I realized I wouldn't know what to do then. I wasn't sure which of us needed rescuing. I reached into my back pocket for Nikki's phone number and found it with the list of discussion questions for my job as graveyard cashier. I stopped walking and stood on a speed bump in the middle of the street. In a nearby trailer, I could see the morning news flickering through the blinds, and somewhere a little farther away, I heard the hum of a car warming up, and thinking of Cather, I thought, *good people in flimsy shelters*. I imagined coming back far in the future to find Nikki married, surrounded by children, waving her apron at me. She could be my Ántonia, but then who would that make me?

I took the papers, which were growing sweaty in my hands, and began tearing them in neat halves, again and again, until I could hardly grip the tiny clump that remained. There didn't seem to be much wind, but as I tossed it into the air, the pieces swirled up and back at me, landing on my shoulders like confetti.

KNUCKLES

When I was fifteen, my brothers and I stole our father's pet buffalo, but before I get too far into that, I need to start with the case against my father:

1) My father loved Knuckles—that was the buffalo's name—more than his children. I have four brothers, but in spite of our number, we filled the landscape around the buffalo like cheap sideshows. My father's primary energies were devoted to its care. He even built an addition onto the house (Knuckles was housebroken at an early age), and the picture that adorned his desk was not of him and his sons on a fishing trip or at a baseball game or even of him with our mother. Rather, it was of Knuckles, seated at the kitchen table on his third birthday, his bowl of dry cereal spilled out before him, a party hat on his head.

2) My father was fond of botched idioms, such as "When the tough get going, wear it" and "If the shoe fits, make hay." His favorite: "People in glass houses shouldn't throw shit at fans." He often quoted these in the presence of company.

3) My father was incapable of small talk without giving unsolicited advice.

4) My father turned our small ranch into a tourist attraction.

5) At stock and western shows, he often waxed his mustache and wore a t-shirt that read:

`MY DANCE PARTNER IS HAIRIER THAN I AM.`

6) Three weeks before we took the buffalo, my father skipped the twins' final high school football game to tend to Knuckles, who was sick with flu-like symptoms (although the veterinarian assured him it was probably a simple case of dietary indiscretion). It wouldn't be that noteworthy, except that it was the playoffs and we lived in Texas.

* * *

The night of the game, I remember hoping our father would show up. My mother was there, but as you're probably beginning to see, this isn't really about her.

I am the youngest of the brothers, preceded in order by a set of twins, Adam and Aaron, and two middle children, Ben and Chris. We all have ordinary names, and in our own unique ways, have probably spent years trying to overcome them.

At the time of the game, I was a freshman, but due to my size, I was starting on the offensive line. Back then, I weighed in at just shy of three hundred pounds if I'd eaten a light lunch, and my girth was useful even if I struggled to wrangle opposing speed rushers. I posed an obstacle. My brothers filled more glamorous positions—fullback, tight end, linebacker. We weren't outstanding, but we played with abandon, and on most evenings, we were worth watching.

I won't bore you with the details of the game, although I remember most of them. We ended up losing by a fourth-quarter field goal. But it was our father I meant to tell you about. Throughout the game, I kept looking into the home stands, hopeful that he might materialize, but when

Central's quarterback took the final knee, he was nowhere to be seen. He had missed all but two games that year, mostly for Knuckles-related reasons. On senior night, he came but brought the buffalo and stood off the far end of the track, grazing him. The children flocked from both sides, and the state troopers helped corral traffic like Christmas elves.

After the game, I patted the twins on the shoulder pads as we headed off. They kept glancing toward the stands. I looked down to where our silhouettes made slanted X's on the track in front of us. Adam, no. 53, looked back at me and said, "Motherfucker." Nothing else.

As I try to trace the idea of kidnapping Knuckles back to its genesis, the football game is where I end up, but I know it had long been building. In my history class, I was learning about the French Revolution, about how 18th century France was ripe for bloodlust. And in natural sciences, I was learning geysers are created when a bottom layer of subterranean water is superheated and constricted until it pushes to the surface and explodes in a cloud of steam.

I was barely pulling Cs in both classes, but that doesn't mean I wasn't learning anything.

* * *

Why everyone loved Knuckles:

1) He danced. My father had taught him somewhere early on, although he refused to admit it. He said that Knuckles naturally loved it and pointed out how he pouted when my father didn't oblige. We often came home to them dancing—as we did after the playoff game. His hooves were up on our father's shoulders and there was music playing. All our father said was, "Look who's feeling better."

2) He made you feel guilty. I'll admit he was cute in his strange, buffalo way, but the power was in his eyes; they contained volumes of history. When I was young, I learned about the great slaughters on the Plains and about how you could follow the railroads, hopping from one carcass to another, without ever touching the ground. Knuckles was a living memorial.

3) We lived in Texas, a land of mythical scale and appetite. Its people do not fear superlatives. My father hung a wooden sign above Knuckles's door proclaiming, HOME OF THE LARGEST PET IN NORTH AMERICA, and people came to see it. They toured his room and fell in love with the idea that he was part of our family. They laughed at my father's description of how Knuckles sometimes stayed in his room all day and only came out "to potty." Then they laughed again as he added, "Just like all my other teenagers."

4) He was photogenic. In addition to the picture on my father's desk, when the tourists came, we would dress Knuckles up in various tailored costumes. You could get your picture taken as his bride, or as his Native hunter, or even—for a limited time—as his little brother.

5) He was a celebrity, and after a certain point, that alone is enough to win over a good many people. There was even talk of a television special at one point, but it was to be done by a low-budget network that got bought out.

* * *

As with most crimes, the abduction of Knuckles was a crime of opportunity. Shortly after football season, my father made the decision to expand Knuckles' enclosure. The old fencing was battered and needed to be replaced (Knuckles tended to be hard on it, especially during mating season). But since he couldn't bear to sequester the buffalo entirely within his room, he planned it to coincide with a small country and western exposition in Amarillo. It was a small affair—one that he'd been to several years running and thought we could handle. "Give them the typical spiel, but don't demonstrate the dancing," he said. "We need them to come out here to see more."

Here is the scene where my brothers and I conspire around a bonfire:

We had been making s'mores and complaining about Knuckles—as we were prone to doing.

"What I don't get," Aaron said, "is how he's not making more profit off that stupid thing.

He spends everything he brings in on the buffalo. Why can't he expand the house for us?"

The twins were still sharing a room, even though they were seniors.

"Motherfucker," Adam said.

"And it's not like *we're* getting anything from him," Chris said.

We catalogued the injustices. Ben was still bitter that we couldn't ski behind him (as we'd done for one glorious day the summer before when we found water skis at a local yard sale and made Knuckles pull us around the pasture). Our father had declared that, due to our size, it exhausted Knuckles.

Chris complained that our mother always allied herself with our father, with Knuckles. "I don't get it," he said. "Why did they have us if he was always going to be their favorite?"

Everyone looked at me as though I had something to add. I couldn't help but feel a little flattered. Even though

I played football with them, it had only been recently that they'd included me in their bonfires, their weekly retreat from all things buffalo. I thought about how a buffalo in captivity was likely to live only about twenty-five years.

Instead, I said, "I hate him."

"Me too," they echoed.

"Motherfucker," Adam said again, as though this decided something.

* * *

For the show, our father gave us full use of the truck and trailer. He gave us money for gas and a motel room and wished us well. As he watched, we gently led the buffalo into the trailer.

All of us insisted on going, and our father supported it. I think he imagined the trip would be a sort of bonding. The truck was a quad-cab, but with our collective size, it left me—the youngest—to ride in the back and keep an eye on the buffalo. Amarillo wasn't that far away. Had we gone there, it would have only taken a few hours, but the plan was to go beyond it, to take him to a slaughterhouse across the state line.

As we drove, I lay down in the bed, putting my legs just to the side of the fifth wheel. It was still early in the day, and the wind that whipped over the top of the cab was freezing. It's a popular misconception that big people don't get cold. I had a couple heavy blankets and a thermos of tea, but it hardly helped. I envied Knuckles's coat. While we'd arranged a code for me to communicate when I got too cold or tired, I didn't want to use it, but instead hunkered down to listen to Knuckles shift his weight around in the trailer.

At a gas station partway there, I told the others I needed to defrost for a while, and Chris offered to swap with me.

26

"New plan," Adam said once we were on the road again. "We're going to sell him."

I waited for more details, but that was pretty much it.

And I want to say at this point that while my brothers aren't heartless, I'll concede they're sometimes dense. I finally got from them the sale location—an interstate rest stop near the Oklahoma line. It was a famous tourist trap and featured two things of note: a thirty-foot-high statue of a rodeo cowboy aboard a bronco and a Texas flag so large it couldn't properly be flown at half-mast without dragging the ground. I'd been there twice before, both times with my father.

* * *

Things I told my father from the pay phone at the rest stop (with my brothers hovering near my shoulder):

1) Knuckles has been taken.
   (Aaron's words)

2) You never cared about finding us before this.
   (Adam's words)

3) Things are going to be different from now on.
   (Ben's words)

4) Do you have any final words for Knuckles?
   (Chris's words)

My brothers had elected me to handle the call because, as the youngest, they felt I had the least to complain about and could relay messages without getting worked up. They circled around me as I talked, and I shielded the receiver from them. I had expected the conversation to be more fraught with tension like the ransom calls in movies, but we had no clear list of demands. We merely wanted our father to know that we were ridding our family of Knuckles and that there was nothing he could do about it.

For the most part, he received the news calmly, although I could tell by the silences between questions that he was upset. He wanted to know where we were and what we were up to. He said, "Texas isn't as big as you think."

When I repeated this to the others, Adam let out a hoot. "Motherfucker!" he said. "It's on."

Ben grabbed for the phone and began to mimic an auctioneer selling a buffalo, but I shrugged him off. I was—at least for a moment—glad to be physically bigger than my brothers. I told him he was an idiot, and remarkably, the others agreed.

My father said, "Please don't harm Knuckles," and there was a long silence on the other end of the line. For a moment, no one said anything. My brothers leaned over me trying to hear, but with the interstate noises beyond us, their efforts were useless. When the silence continued, I realized our father might be crying, and while I couldn't have said why, this angered me. I looked at my brothers, mere inches from me, and felt emboldened. I shouted into the phone, "Why didn't you see this coming?" and hung up.

My brothers laughed and clapped me on the back. When they asked me what he had said, I told them he was going on and on about how he knew every buffalo rancher in the tri-state and how, if we didn't knock it off, he was going to call the police. The twins found it funny.

"I would love to see the police get involved in this," Aaron said.

* * *

The truth was that none of us quite understood how to go about what we were doing. We were open to suggestions.

The tourist trap helped. They kicked us out soon after we parked outside the lines and up against the curb, and we were forced instead to set up shop one exit down in an abandoned lot next to a gas station. There were no trees, just high grass and a perimeter of brightly colored campaign signs. *Guy for Sheriff!* one read. Ben insisted on keeping that one standing, but we took the rest down and fashioned a couple of our own that read, *Yes! The buffalo is for sale.*

We parked the trailer in the middle of the lot and stood by its side like bowling pins. We waited, but no one stopped.

"Do you suppose Knuckles needs a walk?" I finally asked, but no one moved.

I opened the back of the trailer and grabbed Knuckles's lead. He was surprisingly agile. Buffalo in general appear much clumsier than they actually are, but even so, I hadn't expected him to be capable of such power and grace so soon after confinement. We took a couple laps around the lot before stopping for a bathroom and snack break near the gas station dumpsters. At the pumps, a few people stared and took pictures, but most were nonplussed. He ate for several minutes, creating a clearing in the grass. I remembered from school what our teachers had said about buffalos being nomadic, about their need for constant movement.

After he finished, I picked some stray chaff out of his beard and we took a few more laps before Knuckles pulled me back toward his captors, who were busy playing poker like a set of rodeo clowns.

* * *

Reasons for not running away from home:

1) We all loved football.

2) We believed we needed each other, and our collective mass created something we didn't think we could move.

3) In spite of the hoopla surrounding the buffalo, the wooden gate at the end of our lane still read "Lewis & Sons" and loomed as a distant promise.

4) The presence of injustice and oppression.

5) Our adolescent fascination with such themes and our eagerness to define ourselves against them.

* * *

We waited through the midday heat without much success. We were growing sweaty and bored. My brothers tried to strike up the old conversation about how much we hated the buffalo, but it fizzled after a couple of minutes. One man finally did stop by. He wore a cowboy hat with the word STUD stenciled across the front. He was young and curious if the sign was for real.

When we confirmed it, he laughed, said "Right on!" and moved next door to pump some gas.

For lunch, we sent Chris to buy a pile of snack food from the convenience store. He came back with three bags of potato chips, a few boxes of Little Debbies and a case of Dr. Pepper. We sat and ate in silence. The soda was warm and unsatisfying. I kept watching for our father but decided after a while that scrutinizing traffic is the sort of activity that can make a person go insane. A couple of sheriff deputies passed by, but they didn't seem to consider us any kind of nuisance.

Toward evening, a serious buyer did arrive. Rather than pulling through the driveway, he hopped the curb in his pickup. It felt like an announcement of intentions. We all stood up and flapped our shirts in unison. Knuckles continued lounging on his stomach.

* * *

From here, the story is hard to tell. I've concocted other happier or more poetic endings:

1) Our father through intuition and love for his buffalo—which acts as a homing device in such moments—arrives at the lot to a charging Knuckles. We and the buyer are in his path, and our father is forced to shoot his beloved buffalo to save his other sons.

2) The buyer is a Native and we sell the buffalo to him with the confidence that somehow what we've done has been redeemed, that we are noble and in harmony with the universe.

3) Bored, we tell the buyer the sign's a joke. He laughs—like the stud did—and we all return home.

*　*　*

If you like one of those, you can stop here, although none of them happened. Our father did eventually arrive, but I might not get to that part. Instead, I give you the scene with the buyer:

The man dismounted his pickup and looked our way. From a distance, he called out "Howdy" but kept his eyes trained on Knuckles as he walked closer. When he reached us, he shook each of our hands without giving a name, as though we'd already reached an agreement.

"That's a pretty docile buffalo you have there," he said.

"It is," Aaron said. "Domesticated even."

The man grunted. He rolled his lips around in a way that suggested he was accustomed to chewing and spitting things.

For a moment, none of us said anything. Everyone stared at Knuckles and watched him swish his tail in the heat. Then, as if sensing his cue, he rolled onto his back, threw his legs in the air, and ground his shoulders into the dirt. A cloud of dust blew our way, and we all turned away or covered our faces—everyone, that is, except the man, who kept watching. After a minute or so, Knuckles settled back onto his belly, somehow satisfied.

"How much for the hair?" the man asked.

My brothers and I looked at each other. "Say again?"

"The hair. The pelage." He stepped forward and gently ran his hand through Knuckles's coat. Up close, the man smelled like tobacco and corned beef.

Somewhere I'd learned that dogs are capable of at least a hundred expressions, and although I was conflicted about Knuckles, I believed he was intelligent, capable of at least twenty. I looked to him for clairvoyance.

Before I could say anything, Chris asked, "Why don't you want the whole buffalo?"

It lingered as an accusation until Aaron said, "Five hundred dollars."

The man laughed. It sounded nothing like the stud. "I'll give you ten dollars a pound."

"Okay," Adam said, "What do we need to do?"

* * *

We followed the man to a nearby ranch. We weren't scared at this point and had no reason to be. We were pretty big, and in spite of the man's cryptic intentions, we were finally accomplishing something that resembled our original intention.

"Motherfucker!" Adam yelled out the window to passing traffic.

Aaron drummed on the dashboard and revved the truck at stop signs.

Ben and Chris grinned like idiots.

At his ranch, he had us lead Knuckles into a loading chute that dead-ended into the side of a pole barn. Knuckles was so used to being handled that he didn't object. The rancher tied Knuckles's muzzle to a bar above his head and tethered his legs to the sides. He asked, "Ever shaved him before?"

We said we hadn't.

"It's November, so the pelage is as thick as it's going to get. After we do this, you'll probably need to slaughter him or keep in a barn the rest of the winter."

A couple of my brothers laughed. "Can we help?" Adam asked. And the rancher was glad to let us.

* * *

Reasons you should never shave a buffalo:

1) There's a lot more hair than you probably realize. It's messy and time-consuming, even with several helpers. There's over a foot of hair on a buffalo's head and over eight inches on the breast (the rancher measured). The tail has almost twenty inches.

2) Only a professional should do such things, one accustomed to the buffalo's fidgeting and discomfort.

3) It's not natural.

4) In shaving, you may see a side of your co-workers that frightens you. My brothers worked with sloppy glee, cutting large chunks from the flanks and hindquarters. As it fell onto the tarp below, they laughed and worked faster. And they shaved the beard and head, even though the man said that hair was too coarse for his purposes.

5) A buffalo's coat is its glory. Without it, a buffalo looks pathetically bovine and dispossessed. When finished, its bare hump will look like a burden, and its inability to raise its head above its shoulders will suddenly break your heart.

* * *

When we were finished, and the hair had been gathered up, it was late. The rancher offered us the old bunkhouse for the night, and we accepted. "We can sell the buffalo tomorrow," my brothers said and helped brush the hair off each other.

I tried to sleep but kept thinking of my father. I imagined him alone in our house, quietly hunched over his desk, paying bills, or alternately, out somewhere on the road, anticipating a reunion with Knuckles. I imagined him straightening the furniture and readying his bed, caring for the animal even in his absence. It was a compassion I was only now beginning to understand.

Somewhere in the night, taunted by my brothers' enthusiastic snoring, I gave up and went back out to the barnyard. The moon was full, and it was easy to find my way. Knuckles was still contained in the makeshift arrangement where we'd left him. The rancher hadn't wanted to test his fencing. "This ranch was built for horses and cattle," he said, "not beasts."

I approached from behind and Knuckles tried to turn his head so he could see me better, but the chute was too narrow. I climbed up to where I could untie him. I squeezed in front of him and slowly backed him down the chute. With no hair surrounding them, his horns stuck out like forklift prongs, less than a foot from my body. Growing up as I did, I'd heard stories of people being gored by buffalo, even ones they'd raised from infancy. And for that reason, my father had seldom let us get too close to Knuckles. He wanted to protect everyone involved, including himself.

So when Knuckles nudged my back mid-walk, I nearly panicked. I had a brief flash of my death, of how gruesome and appropriate it might be. I knew I was powerless. I tried to put it out of mind, but when he did it harder a moment later, I dropped the lead and backed against the fence, squaring off with Knuckles. "It wasn't me," I said but knew this wasn't true. I was complicit. I had hated and condemned him. I had sinned against my father and now this beast would enact whatever vengeance was due. I closed my eyes.

His silence was more menacing than his horns. There was a long pause before Knuckles began coming toward me, but he didn't charge. His hoofs scratched the dirt, and I heard his breath as he drew close. As the first hoof hit the fence behind me, the rails shook, and Knuckles grunted. Even though it was becoming clear what he wanted, he seemed to be asking. I opened my eyes and felt his weight shift onto my shoulder. I could've helped him with the second hoof, but I didn't. Instead, I braced myself against the fence and waited. And although I'd danced with girls only a handful of times, I somehow knew what to do. When he was ready, I reached out and accepted his generosity.

CAKEWALK

You first see her at Polish Town Polka Days. She's the one in mismatched costume, dancing confidently with men twice her age and singing aloud. She is, in this moment, a poster child for the chamber of commerce, for sunlit, Midwestern towns and meat stew. She's not what you'd consider your type, although lately "your type" has become a fading illusion, something you can no longer articulate to yourself, its possessive quality an absurdity. When she passes you, she winks either at you or the red-faced accordion player behind you. You can't tell for sure, and that may be part of what makes an impression.

For the next week at work, you think back on the way she danced—more arms than legs—and the ridiculous outfit—that of a wannabe Swiss maiden. You're sure you'll never see her again.

* * *

You don't believe in serendipity, in soul mates, in love at first sight. Maybe you should. You're worth it.

* * *

The next time you see her, you're at a bland festival in the town of Stacy, an hour from the Twin Cities. There's no theme, only a light spoofing of the spelling of "Days," as in "Stacy Daze." It reminds you of someone you went to high school with, the girl with the hairspray that once caught fire during a candlelight vigil. This is what you're thinking of when you see her again. She's eating cotton candy, a large, pink wad of it. You watch her from afar, not sure it's her. You divide your time between eating and reconnaissance. And there's a water fight in progress. They've backed the town's two fire trucks up against each other and are spraying at a giant red ball on a wire, the type they put on power lines near airstrips to keep planes from hitting them. Neither team seems to be winning, but you watch anyway, convinced that if you're patient, something will happen.

You feel a surge of adrenaline. You've never imagined a scenario, or at least you've never dared to admit it to yourself. You might have confessed to more innocent fantasies of bumping elbows with a reserved and like-minded bookworm in the library, or sharing neighboring seats on a crowded bus, or even getting stood up on a blind date and meeting an attractive woman in the exact same situation. That sort of serendipity could be wished for, even expected, but not this.

And it's not what you thought she'd look like, but it must be her. You recognize it the third time you see her, at Montevideo's Fiesta Days, a celebration of the town's improbable namesake and sister city in Uruguay. You see her at the coronation as she watches from stage left. She wears a dress that reminds you more of a pioneer woman than a Spanish courtesan. She looks misplaced in her costume, but even in more casual clothing, you began to believe you could pick her out of a crowd.

*   *   *

This is how you've reached this point: you lived previously in a world that doesn't exist in most imaginations or in some road atlases. Your hometown has one flashing yellow light and a high school. You were a farmer's firstborn, the one who was supposed to stay, to keep the family on the land, but you neglected—in your father's words—"your duty" and emigrated to the cities for an entry-level job as a filing clerk for the city of St. Paul.

This is the world you've chosen, and yet, it doesn't suit you fully. You remain of the land, of the soil, and on the weekends, the land draws you out. You travel to towns that remind you of the one you left in Iowa. You tell yourself it is ironic. You tell yourself you do this to remind yourself why you left. You tell yourself you do it to marvel at the people in the countryside, the ones decked out for their annual festivals, their enthusiasm masking the undeniable farce.

You tell yourself many things, but don't believe most of them.

At the singles parties you sometimes attend, you've begun lying and telling people you're an architect or an aspiring Olympian. Once, you said you were working on the annex to the Mall of America, but it got you in trouble, and you had to reach deep into your shallow reservoir of architectural knowledge and mall composition to rescue yourself. And another night, you claimed to be an all-American pole-vaulter who worked at Home Depot, only to discover the woman asking—a sandy-blond from White Bear Lake— had been a champion pole-vaulter in college.

Face it, you think, others have more exciting lives. Face it, you think, others are better liars.

You take up smoking. You try karaoke. You begin to imagine your life will take shape if you just meet the right girl. It's the sort of hooey you rejected back in Iowa, but there the women were burly, sported uniform hairstyles. Here, the women are marginally more exotic, and one of them, you believe, might find you worthy.

* * *

On the other hand, you have stopped lying to your father. He still calls sometimes, but only when he has business to discuss. Inevitably, your departure left loose ends, and he calls to straighten them out. He asks after your car, your removal from the family health insurance. Your mother asks about things left in your room and in the communal storage spaces. Can she get rid of your roller blades? Your lava lamp? Your old winter coat? It was a hand-me-down to begin with. The school's having a coat drive. She's getting an exchange student, she tells you, a petite Japanese girl with a name she can't yet pronounce. She needs to put her in your room. At church, everyone asks about you and how you like your new job. She's embarrassed, she says, that she's not sure what to tell them.

At work, you've befriended the stranger of the office's characters. You eventually confess the happenings with the mystery woman to Ashua, a yogi originally from Boulder. Given your roots, you can't bring yourself to seek a more professional mystic. And while you don't share her beliefs, you find your beliefs are changing.

"I don't understand why I keep seeing her," you tell Ashua.

"What is she doing when she appears in your life?" she asks.

The word *appears* bothers you. It makes it sound as if you've dreamt everything. You tell her so.

"Did or didn't. What difference would it make?" she asks. She is always asking questions.

"When I see her, she's usually watching. Sometimes she eats, and once, she was dancing."

"Do you dance?"

"No," you say. "I don't." It's a touchy subject; you've had friends and acquaintances condemn you for it as though it's a character flaw, as though you can't laugh.

Ashua merely nods, but it stings. Then, something that surprises you: she smiles. "I think maybe you are falling in love with yourself."

* * *

You don't take her seriously. This is about soul mates. This is about disproving your father's assertion: "There are a dozen women a man could be perfectly happy with." You've always been a romantic, and you're determined to stay so.

The next few weeks, you go to festivals, but the woman is not there, and as a result, the festivals fade and blur in your memory almost as soon as they've happened. Nothing about them seems new or innovative. Then, just as you begin to think you've outgrown your new world, you head for the Bunyan Bonanza. It's a last-ditch effort. It's upstate, and so you work a half-day on Friday and drive north, beating traffic while listening to Muddy Waters.

As you come into town, you enter a world that resembles your old hometown. It is what some might call a hamlet. Its skyline consists of a handful of church steeples, a water tower, and a grain elevator. You expect to see a lumber mill or two. You expect to see the Paul Bunyan statue looming at the edge of town like a sentry.

You do pass Paul on the way in, just past a set of fast-food restaurants and retail stores, and since you have the time, you stop to stretch. Signs greet you: "Welcome to Paul's Patio," "For events, please make reservations," and "No loitering." And closer to the statue: "Caution: In summer, Paul may become too hot to touch."

There are two women there, working silently. One looks like your aunt, at least from her profile. You watch her as she plants limp American flags around the edge of the cement. Tomorrow, this will be the center of things.

Neither woman acknowledges you.

You proceed toward Paul and examine him in the fading light. You're aware that both Bemidji and Brainerd have larger statues, but there's something compelling about this version, a pose that has him kneeling to the masses, leaning on his axe handle and extending a hand as though he's lifting water from a creek. It's a gesture of cordiality, you suppose, but it's one that's hard to accept from such a large creation. Even in his crouch, he's nearly thirty feet tall. His hand is three feet wide. It says so on a plaque beside his axe blade.

He's hairier than you anticipated. His metal beard extends to the top of his shirt front and obscures his Adam's apple. Hair covers his arms and peeks out of the top of his shirt. Elsewhere, it's clothes—a hat, suspenders, and a trademark flannel shirt. You approach cautiously and run your hand over the worn place in his palm where visiting couples have their pictures taken. You've read about this online.

The woman who resembles your aunt clears her throat behind you, and you turn. "We're not letting him talk today," she says.

You nod, confused.

"Normally, he talks, welcomes you to his patio, imparts wisdom, and so forth, but we're letting him rest up for the big day tomorrow."

You had no idea.

"He'll be back on tomorrow. Would you like me to take your picture?" she asks. She makes a camera motion with her hands for emphasis.

"I don't have a camera," you say. It's a lie, but you're not ready to be here, to document this. "And besides, I don't think he's having his best day."

She nods and resumes her work.

You face Paul again, and for lack of anything more creative, you attempt to shake his hand before turning to leave.

* * *

Your hometown used to have a festival—something called "the Festival of Flags." It was surprisingly global in its conception, and for the weekend, the town park would fill with tents and campers, and the sky would fill with kites. Norwegian, Swiss, German, Irish, Dutch. It was a celebration of similar origin and common destiny, a festival celebrating the journey made by most of the area's residents, homesteaders who came and plowed the prairie and resumed lives much like the ones they'd left behind in Europe.

You remember it fondly, but at the time, you wanted nothing to do with it, with the parade. Your father mandated that your family participate, and so you had to dress in ludicrous Danish clothes you'd never seen anyone in your family wear, even in old photographs. It seemed like the same sort of patriotism and nationalism that made your father hum the school fight song on Friday nights as he washed up after milking. You never understood, and at parades and football games, you reluctantly participated, but you didn't wave and didn't cheer. Always, you felt your father's judgment. He said, "You need to believe in things bigger than yourself."

And that was when you told him to go to hell and received the only slap he ever gave you.

* * *

The next day, the festivities begin with a parade, but you're up before that. You leave "Babe's Lodgings"—a motel littered with pictures of the blue ox—and head to the firehouse for a pancake breakfast. You've done your research, and among other things, this festival has promised that "you can eat and eat and eat." And, if you're honest, this excites you.

The man working the griddle is a performer of sorts, and as soon as you have a plate, he begins slinging pancakes across the garage. "Tell me when!" he yells, and everyone claps as you catch the first two. You miss the next two and tell him to stop after you catch a third. A mismatched set of dogs materialize from under the folding tables in front of you to clean up the drops.

You sit down beside a man wearing a shirt that reads: "Nothing beats fatherhood except hunting." There are no children nearby, and you don't know how to interpret this sign.

The pancakes are dry but delicious with syrup. It's been months since you've had a good flapjack.

At work, your sense of humor has worn thin with colleagues. Ashua is the only one who still has patience with you. She indulges the stories you tell and the pictures you bring back from your travels. No one else does. Chip, your appointed mentor, looks over your most recent ones with disdain. "I've been to Eau Claire before," he says. "Looks about the same as when I left it."

And this is a moment you'll remember: You press him. "But don't you think the festival is sort of, you know, weird?"

Chip stands up from behind his desk. He's a large man, an ex-athlete who doesn't always know what to do with his hands. "Let me tell you what's weird," he says, and you know you're in trouble. "One: It's weird that you still wear shirts with buttonholes in the collar. Two: It's weird that you have no idea what 'business casual' means. And three: I think it's weird that you keep taking these trips when it's the same story week after week, place after place."

You take the pictures from his desk. You're shamed, not by the content or cruelty of his comments, but by your lack of a response. You're supposed to be assertive. You say, "Thanks for taking an interest in me"—something you said a year and a half ago in your job interview and haven't used since.

He's done acknowledging you. You leave as he picks up the phone to order lunch.

At the parade, the floats represent civic groups and churches, small businesses and school groups. Most rely heavily on crepe paper and look like they were assembled in a single afternoon. The route is short enough you hear the high school marching band through the duration of the parade, and the fight song dries like plaster in your ears.

You follow the end of the parade. The last float—a pickup wearing a skirt of cardboard—carries the festival princess toward the patio, toward Paul, her waiting lumberjack. She waves with energy but without discipline. And every few seconds, she leans over to whisper something to the woman sitting next to her.

The names of businesses on the way to the patio delight you: The Woodtick Theatre, The Velvet Antler, The Hairport.

At the patio, the crowds are larger than you expected, but you're overwhelmed by the sensation that she is present. You now recognize the workings of fate in your life.

The rotary club serves lunch. A live, spray-painted blue ox reclines in Paul's shadow. The main event of the afternoon is the lumberjack showdown, a contest of masculinity that pits a red-flannel team against a blue-flannel team. You watch. You scan the crowd.

During the first event, a hybrid contest of tree climbing and axe wielding, you see her on the far side of the crowd. Or you imagine you do. You're not sure until the log-rolling contest down at the pond. You see her. She claps, she cheers, she delights in the absurdity of the contest. You can tell this.

But when you move back to the patio, she disappears, and the crowd closes around you. Meanwhile, the lumberjacks throw axes at targets. They climb taller poles. They take out crosscut saws and work in tandem. They grapple. The crowd cheers, but you're no longer sure what's happening or why it's happening. You don't know the score. And when the teams switch to chainsaws during a crosscut saw contest, you're momentarily afraid until you realize that this is a premeditated part of the show, that the miniature chairs they're tossing into the crowd are meant as souvenirs.

And that's when you see her. She's nearby, just a few people over. She looks disoriented, unimpressed, much like yourself. But when she looks over at you, there is no recognition. She looks through you and beyond you. One of the miniature chairs hits you on the shoulder, and children wash around you, searching for where it landed. The show ends, and the lumberjacks take a bow.

You feel her leave, and when you look back, a plain woman with a baby in a sling has taken her place.

*　*　*

The week before this, your father visited you in the cities. You hadn't been expecting him, but he had wanted to bring you a washer and dryer. You'd recently tried to tell a story about the laundromat to liven up a phone conversation. Your mother took it as a complaint, and someone from church happened to be replacing machines. In other words, they were cheap and working, reason enough for your father to drive eight hours to come see you.

Although you can see your mother's hand in it, she doesn't offer to come. Instead, it is just you and your father. And after the work of moving the appliances is completed, you are forced to pass hours of silence together. The inside of your apartment reveals your spartan nature. You thought your self-discipline and asceticism might please your father, but he gives no indication that it does. Instead, he asks about dinner, and of the available seating, he chooses to sit on a stack of old milk crates. He flips through a road atlas you've left by the couch, already plotting the drive back.

On the way to get something to eat from a local fast-food restaurant, your father comments on the noises your car has been making for months. "You should get that checked out," he says.

"What do you think it is?"

Your father looks at you, and you can sense his disappointment. He says, "Sounds like it's the transmission. Don't you think?"

It feels like it could be a trick question, but you agree.

"Who's your mechanic?" he asks.

Of course you don't have one, unless you count the JVS grads at the local Jiffy Lube. You're forced to admit this, and as a result your father is quiet through most of dinner.

The next day, you offer to show him your office, but he declines. He's eager to make time on the trip back.

*　*　*

After you leave Paul's Patio, you spend the evening in search of her. Even though you don't know her, you imagine a life for her, try to think like she might. But as you do, you're aware that if you overanalyze the situation, you might throw fate an unhittable curveball. If you're meant to be, you think, you'll end up together at the same place. You try to think what you normally do at these festivals, but you can't remember. You're growing disoriented. The crowds drift by you, and you don't know where they're headed.

When you finally spot her, she's blocks ahead of you on Lumberjack Lane, a thoroughfare you've already walked several times. She turns onto a side street and you follow. She walks into church, and you follow. This is where you'll meet her, you decide, which is as it should be. "You should only meet people in places where you could get married," your father always told you.

At the door, a teenager stops you. He wears a hockey jamboree t-shirt and sits behind a collapsible card table.

"Five dollars for the spaghetti," he says. "And three more if you want in on the cakewalk."

You have no idea what a cakewalk is, and he recognizes this.

"Think of it as if a game of musical chairs and a bake sale had a kid together and named it Raffle," he says. This feels rehearsed. "You walk around a circle while the music plays, and then, when it stops, they draw a number, and you're standing by that number, you get to take home a baked good. The proceeds go to Little Wolves Hockey."

He looks at you in assessment. The ten wavers in your hand. You hardly know how it got there. "You've sold me," you say and walk away before he can give you your two dollars.

You follow the signs and wind up in the church's basement—a narrow fellowship hall dominated by orange-yellow carpet and metal folding tables. Along one wall, a set of translucent windows glow from the setting sun. Only a few of the tables are filled. The woman is nowhere to be seen.

A man intercepts you and tells you he's glad you've come. He asks for your name, hometown, and occupation. He's a large man with a firm handshake and skin the color of pie crust. You assume by his cheerfulness that he's some kind of pastor. He gestures toward the food. He says, "Eat inside or out," and hands you a tray.

You take it and try to avoid making eye contact.

"Have at it," he says. "The cakewalk's in fifteen minutes."

* * *

The Monday after your father leaves, you go to lunch with Ashua, to a Middle Eastern restaurant around the corner from your office. You are celebrating her promotion, but you don't talk about it. Instead, you rehash all that has happened in your life, and she advises you to let go. "We struggle because we grasp," she says.

But you don't want to hear it. You take your food seriously instead. You devour your falafel in three bites and then eat most of the tomato salad you were supposed to share. She pretends not to notice your gluttony.

"I don't know what to make of it all," you say. You tell her your plans for the Bunyan Bonanza. She listens. You tell her about your father coming to town. And she listens.

You attempt your own truths. You say, "I doubt I'll ever see that woman again." You say, "She's probably gone. The world gives and the world takes." You say, "It's just another missed connection, and everyone has those."

Ashua nods. "We do," she says. "We believe in them though, because the world is large and it helps to see meaning where there possibly is none."

You're astonished at how often Ashua uses the pronoun *we*.

You finish eating. You start to move toward the restroom, but Ashua is not through with her speech. She says, "The truth is, we could find happiness and compatibility with any number of people, but we get in the way of ourselves."

This is more than you wanted. You can feel yourself smirking. You say, "You sound like my father."

She falls silent but looks you in the eye. She says, "You need to forgive your father."

The restaurant is crowded, and you'd rather not make a scene, so instead of arguing, you stand and walk out. She doesn't stop you, and as you pass the front window, you look inside to see her sipping tea, the check still face down on the table in front of her.

*   *   *

Outside the church, you sit along the periphery and sip institutional lemonade. People crowd around the desserts and point out the ones they donated.

You spot her among them as the people scatter to form a rough circle.

The cakewalk begins. On the far side of the circle, an emcee ascends a milk crate and bellows over the music. At first, you don't connect this man with the one in the basement. You stare. You watch. The stereo plays bluegrass, and when the man isn't speaking, he holds the microphone up to the speaker.

You watch her as she dances among the contestants. A surprising number of men participate. They stare at her backside as she dances. There are no holy places where such dancing is done.

You stare. You eat. She catches your eye from across the circle and motions for you to join. You've just now finished your garlic bread, and so you do. You dance near her, trying to discern which of the men is most lascivious, which might be the most appealing to her.

The emcee rhapsodizes about the round's desserts. There's a cheesecake. Cherry dumplings. Something with both chocolate and rhubarb. An apple pie. This round, the emcee announces, will be a marathon round. Then, as you are bracing yourself for purgatory, he reveals he was kidding and stops the record player.

You weren't ready for it. You tumble into the man in front of you. Or nearly do. You sidestep him at the last moment, but as you do, you bump into the table of deserts, knocking it aslant, sending some of the deserts to the lawn, and it's then that you feel the sensation of your foot landing in some sort of pie. It squishes. Your foot slides forward and nearly sends you to the ground. There is a small gasp from those nearby. Everyone turns to look at you. You look at your shoes.

After a pause, as those in charge rush over to salvage what can be salvaged, the announcer reprimands you. He says, "Uh oh, party foul!" He's standing three feet away, and yet he proclaims it into the microphone. The comment was not for you anyway. None of this was. You apologize, and you mean it. A hand claps you on the back. Someone tells you not to worry about it. There's nervous laughter from a group that surrounds the woman who brought the pie. You move away from them and reclaim your old seat away from the circle. You can feel your how red your face is, but you can do nothing about it.

* * *

When she comes to you, she has napkins. Your left shoe is in your hand. This is not how it was supposed to be. She offers her name and the napkins. It's Annie. You didn't know.

"I'm you," you say. At least that's what you think comes out.

She must have heard something. She blushes and proffers the napkins. You wipe at your shoes, but the cinnamon filling smears and refuses to come out of the tread completely.

"I can go back and get your pie," Annie says. "Technically, I think it's yours."

You nod, recognize it for the joke that it is. Yet, she heads back toward the cakewalk, which has resumed in your absence, larger and brighter than before. She comes back with the pie rubble in her hand. "Here," she says.

"Yes, here," you say.

"I should change my shoes," you say. "I have others in my car."

She looks at you. She's quiet and expectant.

"I didn't mean that as any kind of proposition. I just mean I have shoes in my car. And I'm going to go get them."

This is only partly true, of course. You do have shoes but have no plans on changing into them. Now that your moment has arrived, you've botched your lines. Your shoes are messy. The light is fading. A part of you is already in your car driving away. You trust that she'll understand.

"You understand?"

"Sure," she says. "Sure."

And with that, you dismiss her.

* * *

This is the familiar ending where you run away: On Lumberjack Lane, no one seems to notice your flight. It's been a while since anyone has. And yet you feel pursued. You run past the theatre, the bars, the market; a blur of Americana. When you get to your motel, your momentum carries you past it, onward toward the hill.

The events have ended for the night, and Paul's Patio is abandoned.

Nearing Paul, you take him in fully: his oafish smile and unbuttoned flannel shirt, his awful beard. *How could they ever be proud of you?*

You look around. There is no one.

Paul says, "I'm the biggest lumberjack in the world."

Paul says, "I made Mount St. Helens when I piled rocks to put out my campfire."

You close the gap between the two of you and kick Paul in the knee as a sort of experiment. The metal is hollow, and your blow reverberates like a tympani.

Paul says, "Thanks for coming to see me."

You look toward his hand. It's possibly his weakest spot. You climb on and stomp, desperate to wound him, break a finger, to somehow leave a mark.

And after you fail at this, you sink down into his palm, dejected. The night around you is full of sound, cicadas and katydids, bullfrogs down at the pond, and in the distance, music from town. But Paul has nothing more to say. You lie back and let the night continue without you.

You are without plan, open to suggestion.

How, you wonder, do you get to the part where Annie comes for you? How do you get anyone to notice your absence, to track you like a wounded creature, pausing at the places you've been, aware of the pain you must be in? You know it's foolish. You can't help but imagine though, what it might be like now, if she found you here in Paul's hand, if she knew to come, if she had the generosity not to judge. You strain to imagine it to where it's almost real: the confident crunch of gravel, her voice calling out to you, her warm hand on your shoulder. Paul might call out to her in the darkness with something wiser and less egotistical than before, something about love and loyalty and how everything he did would not have been possible without his trusty ox.

The night is timeless. It all might happen, you think. You just have to wait. And so you do. You slide over on Paul's palm, leaving a space for her, and you wait.

LAND OF OPPORTUNITY

I will tell it as it was, except this time we will fall in love.

This is true: in third grade, Ms. Washburn has passed out the colored pencils to the half dozen of us who are too poor or neglected to have such extravagances. The rest of the classroom is filled with kids whose parents have bought them mega-sets, 64 or 128 pencils, in hues and shades we cannot pronounce. You are one of those children.

This is the first of perhaps a hundred turning points. You and I have bonded over lunch, over the Salisbury steak that you refused to eat, that I did eat. We played at recess. All I would have to do is slide my plastic chair a few tiles to the right and borrow from your tiered display, colorful missiles aimed at the suspended ceiling. Ms. Washburn has taught us to share. We have been learning about the Underground Railroad, and she says, "Sometimes all we have to do is be brave and make room. All we have to do is share what we have."

I don't borrow your pencils, not because of the grander implications, but because I am shy, because during recess, I have sweated a great deal, and even though I wear sweatpants, I am damp in strange areas, and I have begun to resign myself to my life sentence as one who perspires, whose movements must remain modest and measured. In short, I am scared you will smell me, that you will rescind any future offers of pencils, of lunch leftovers, of friendship. And so I do not ask. And for the next week, you still look at me and smile, but then it begins to fade.

* * *

In this version of the story, we meet on a Greyhound bus as it barrels through Utah. It is a chance meeting, serendipitous in hindsight. Aren't we constantly creating myths we can vindicate?

I am headed into the slickrock wilderness and have loaded a pack full of high-tech survival equipment made of space-age polymers I struggle to pronounce. And you're there. How could you not be? You sleep with your head against the window, ignoring the man singing aloud two seats back. *Pam, Pam, I want to be your lamb*--unfamiliar lyrics to a tune we all recognize. Everything is dry and different, and when I look out the window, I see we are on the wrong side of the center line, but the road is straight and broad, and I trust somehow we will make it through.

I don't know where you were headed, yet you get off at my stop, and we drink overpriced diner milkshakes beneath a red mesa. After we order, the waitress brings us a single check and encourages us to pay when we're ready.

"I felt led to the desert," I say. "Why are you here?"

"My family is here now," you say. "They've become obsessed with the quality of light."

I take a sip of my milkshake and nod, but you say, "It's no different than any other addiction. It's all just dopamine."

And this, I realize, is a truer statement. From that moment, we make sense to each other, and when, upon rising to leave, I fail to find my pack, I have no choice but to follow you wherever you are going.

* * *

In seventh grade, our classmates develop a social itch. They begin having parties every weekend, a frenzied pace

54

few friendships will be able to survive. But at the idea of it, the world yawns wide with potential. Popularity is a cash grab, and those who host want their turn among the fluttering bills.

At your party, we're not bold enough to play spin the bottle. We are good kids. Most of us are good Christians; our largest sin is gregariousness, and it's believed this will pass.

Instead, we supplant it with a night-time game of hide-and-go-seek, which means everyone pairs off and winds up in the sort of locations that could only be romantic to the novice or the lovesick. One couple hides beneath a spruce tree. The cascade of limbs hides them from our view, but we can still hear their urgent whispering.

"You're it," one of the others says to us as they depart across the wet grass. We both understand it's largely a formality—something that will reassemble only if your parents' car pulls into the driveway. Someone will run from the trees and we will give chase, and appearances will be restored.

As we sit on your porch, you and I are not tempted, even as we hear the unmistakable sounds of the spruce couple stumbling around the bases. At one point, the tree rattles violently, and you startle. I nearly grab your hand, but I don't.

We've talked only marginally over the years. You have had your circles, and I have had mine, but I've noticed you. I can recall several of our encounters—like in fourth grade when we were forced to square dance together during music class, and in sixth when you sat next to me during the monthly movie and caught me crying at the end of *The Mighty Ducks* but didn't make fun of me.

This night, we sit side-by-side once again on a weathered porch swing. Since it doesn't hang from the ceiling, you call it a "glider." When I run out of other things, I say, "I didn't know you showed horses," and it delights you, because in the crush of hormones, no one else seems to have noticed.

You lead me out to the barn, and we look at your horse, Ashes. I say, "Palomino?" because it's one of the few horse breeds I know.

And you say, "Not pure-bred."

We stand and watch her, even though she does nothing remarkable. She lies in a bed of pine shavings on the floor of her stall, closer to the front gate than the back wall. You sit on top of your show box for a better view, and I sit next to you, and our legs press together as though magnetized. The night seems to have conspired for this.

There's nothing more to it. I never reach for you, nor you for me. Even now, I believe it's because we don't know where the others may be hiding. The truth is I'm scared. Already, I have idealized you; you are someone who is sophisticated in a way I will never be.

In hindsight, I see your invitation, and I cringe at its quiet generosity.

* * *

In this version of the story, we are never formally introduced. You are a woman I see once a week at the grocery store, where I work as a low-level manager. I have failed somewhere else and have been put here until I can recognize subtlety.

And how I try: I bring thunder and lightning to the lettuce display so customers will know to step away from the cabbage before the sprinklers erupt. I make elaborate displays of the oranges and pineapples. I liberate the potatoes from their bushel baskets and mound them in a pyramid between the onions and the tomatoes. I import an Astroturf tree and suspend the bananas from its hooks.

You come in on Thursdays and handle the produce so tenderly I can't help but notice you. You wear long-sleeved shirts of soft cotton, and when you think I'm not looking, you polish the apples and re-mound them.

Eventually, you approach me and make requests. You know the names of exotic and seasonal fruits I have to look up in the interim before your next visit. I order star and dragon fruit for you, assorted Asian vegetables and organic grapefruit. Each week you judge my offerings, sometimes taking them and sometimes moving on toward the bakery with an empty cart.

I put out samples, but you are not the type. You seem to know what you want, and I can either provide it or I can't.

* * *

What almost brings us together: junior year, you and I both audition for the school musical *Oklahoma!* I do so reluctantly but have always had a good voice. I am given the lead. You are appointed understudy for Laurey, my love interest. A week into the rehearsals, the lead comes down sick with mono, and you step into the role. You're a better fit for it. I'm not alone in my judgment. Others agree, especially the director, a retired New Yorker. A viral outbreak has saved his show.

We practice every day after school. Some days, you ask for a ride home, and I oblige. Sometimes, on the way to the car, I sing a few bars of "The Surrey with the Fringe on Top." You laugh. You love the absurdity of my unrestored Chevy, what I call The Supernova.

But whatever tension we experience is safely reined in by imagining a silent third passenger, a presence that oscillates between Jesus and your boyfriend.

The latter is in the musical, but after rehearsal, he often has to leave directly for wrestling practice. He's on the team, but he is good enough that they let him miss obscene amounts of practice.

You believe in holy courtship, have read and internalized, *How Dating Nearly Destroyed Me*, a harrowing memoir of a woman who struggled through a set of ill-advised and unhealthy relationships before finding her Christian husband. Even though I think the book is overkill, I believe similarly. I don't believe in premarital passion, the conflation of lust and desire intractable.

And yet, preceding opening night, rumors circulate that, instead of miming the act, I will kiss you on the musical's final night when the script calls for it. This passes for a controversy in our small town, and on that night, I dip you back and almost do—your eyes are closed as though anticipating it—but I stop myself. A great chasm is fixed between what I want and what I think I'm allowed to want.

The crowd loves us, and at an event where a standing ovation is nearly requisite, they give us three, thereby validating our chemistry. We hold hands on stage as we bow, and the rest of the cast urges us forward into a space where only we exist, the audience audible but invisible beyond the spotlights. I spin and dip you, and the crowd whistles and roars. In the receiving line outside the auditorium, children beg to have their picture taken with the two of us.

* * *

In this version of the story, we are campaign workers in Atlanta where we work for an understaffed political bid. We are not supposed to win, but we believe if we stand out on the street and talk with people, they will be won over by our candidate's simple logic and modest sensibilities.

We are assigned to canvass a suburban mall together, and after discretely handing out pamphlets in Macy's and stalking shoppers outside The Limited, we wind up in the food court, eating at Chick-fil-A. The plaque near our table proclaims that this is the first mall food court in the country.

In a fit of inspiration and low blood sugar, we decide to sing and dance to reach more people, to end our day of futility. We become street performers. We do not know each other well, but we've somehow internalized the same melodies, and we recognize when to alter the lyrics to plug our candidate. People stop to listen. They think we want money, and a couple elderly men pass around their hats like offering plates. A crowd gathers. Such spontaneity rarely happens in malls. For the finale, you jump up onto the table and spin around a fake palm tree like a lamp post, and I catch you in my arms. The food court erupts with applause and whistles, and as the security guards lead us away, the employees inside the Sbarro and Panda Express continue to bang metal utensils against the counter, demanding an encore.

* * *

Later, in high school, we are still religious, and we do not go to prom. Instead, we have an all-night soiree, an event coordinated by several local churches and a few sets of ambitious parents. It is a night devoid of drinking, dancing, and all other forms of debauchery. You attend with your boyfriend.

We roller skate. We putt-putt. A local steakhouse donates a group room and we cram in, thirty-five people in strange, underdeveloped costumes we spend much of the night explaining to one another. "I'm a 1970s Cleopatra," you say, and I nod, even though I think it's a lame and incomprehensible concept. You are wearing an antique bridesmaid dress, puffy in the sleeves and open around the neck. It is the color of Pepto-Bismol. It is a monstrosity.

But I can hardly cast stones. I am dressed as an impoverished Sherlock Holmes. I carry a pipe and wear a deerstalker on my head, but my coat is threadbare, and nothing about me is particularly urbane or sophisticated.

You nod at me and say, "Nice hat" when we are seated across from each other at dinner. Your boyfriend, who has eschewed costume, sits to your right, and when he knows I am looking, he puts a lean arm around you and squeezes your shoulders.

* * *

This time we will meet at a bowling alley in Missouri. We won't know the other is there until the tornado warning is announced. As we cram ourselves behind the sturdy desk near the shoe rentals, you ask, "What exactly is in those aerosol cans?" meaning the ones they use to disinfect and deodorize shoes. Several of us laugh. You didn't come alone, but since this is my version of the events, I edit out the bachelorette party with their hats and straws fashioned to look like genitalia, and I put you next to me, the smells of pinewood and community shoes all around us. When the radar clears, you join me for a few frames. We are all so grateful to be alive that the owner lets us all bowl for free. The backlights come on, and the balls grow luminous. After all the jokes about shoes, you forsake them and bowl in your socks, which glow like tiny UFOs. The balls charge the pins head-on and split them with thunder.

I say to you, "I wonder how long it would take to get really good at this." I say to you, "I can't think of a cleaner example of cause and effect." I say to you, "What are you doing after this?"

You say, "One thousand hours." You smile. You say, "You're an odd one." You laugh. You say, "I take my evenings one hour at a time."

When the pins jam, we cannot find anyone to help and therefore I must slip-skate down our lane, all the while unsure of what will need to be fixed and how I will go about it.

* * *

This is the part I cannot revise.

When we sneak away from the all-night soiree, we take my car, but I let you drive. It's a stick shift, so this is the lie we tell ourselves at first: I am teaching you to drive.

You've deceived your boyfriend. You've told him you're going to be outside gazing at stars and talking with a female friend. He is probably off roughhousing with his buddies. And I am with you.

This is the feeling of flying I was warned I'd have, a surreal intersection of fantasy and reality. We are renegades and adulterers. We have departed from the group, and the independence feels fresh and overwhelming. We don't know where else to go, so we end up at a 24-hour gas station across town. We go inside to buy cappuccinos even though neither of us drinks coffee. I convince you that tonight is a night for first attempts, that it takes fifteen times to establish a habit, that this camouflaged version hardly constitutes coffee. You appeal to the cashier for a second opinion.

"Pumpkin spice or English toffee?" you ask, even though you have already made up your mind. You simply want someone to confirm with authority the things you have already decided.

"Pumpkin spice," he says.

Outside, you take a sip and burn your tongue. You say, "I should sue."

You continue to drive. We pull out of the gas station and onto a side street. At the stop sign a half-block away, you stall the car twice. I offer encouragement, and when that doesn't work, I gently lift the slack in your dress to demonstrate how you have to ease off the clutch. "Like this," I say, and you smile. "Like this," I say.

You put your hand on mine, pressing it against your leg. The moment is thick with humidity. Something has been decided. I move my hand further up your leg. You don't push it away and your hand remains on mine. With my other hand, I reach up and touch the nape of your neck, and we are about to kiss when a man opens the door behind you and climbs into the back seat.

My faith proves to be a loose winter coat—well-made but fitted for someone else. The shift in winds catches me exposed.

Previously, we had held discussions about theodicy. We knew there was evil in the world and believed it could manifest itself in mysterious accordance with God's will. It was always a possibility. We had been taught that we were all sinners and that severity of sin didn't matter, that we were all part of a network of failures, and that relating to other members was as simple as triangulation, locating the connection between us and them, between them and God.

But we never had the chance that night.

When the man climbed in and showed us the gun, he didn't ask, "So you're Christians?" He didn't ask, "What are you doing out this late?" He didn't notice our strange attire or the cross dangling from my rearview mirror. Or if he did, he never indicated it. Instead, all he said when he climbed in was, "Drive." And this time, when you lifted your foot from the clutch, the car shot forward gracefully, and we were off.

* * *

This is real: the man rides in the back and calls out directions. Even though you drive, he keeps the gun aimed loosely at me. I wish I were driving. I wish I were braver. I wish I weren't a pacifist. I am a fool.

He orders us onto streets that surely would have been familiar during the day, but at night and in this context, belong to a foreign country. The man sits in the back and hums a song we both recognize. Neither of us looks at him directly, but I want to. He is young and smells like shaving cream. Next to him sits a duffel bag.

After a while, he begins fidgeting and drumming on the seat. He sets the gun down to do this, but you keep driving. It's difficult to see him in the shadows of the backseat, in the flicks of streetlight. I only look once and when I do, he lurches forward and smacks me. Then, as if seeing your dress for the first time, he fingers the ridiculous taffeta of it.

My face still stings and so I try not to look. You continue to drive, as commanded. He tugs at the loose top of your bridesmaid dress until your breasts are exposed. How do I know? I simply do. His hands play at your nipples and cup your breasts. He laughs as you cringe. He says, "Just a little fun. I'm harmless." His hands slide over your throat, your sternum, your breasts. His touch is entirely wrong. You look resolutely ahead. As he molests you, he keeps giving directions and somehow you keep driving. There are no stoplights or stop signs at which to stall, to somehow change our awful momentum. Finally, I find some wherewithal and say, "Please. Stop." You momentarily brake, as though I was talking to you. "Drive," he says, and when you do, he reaches across the seat and flicks me in the crotch, where my ill-fitting pants have made a tent he must have taken for an erection. You scream at the suddenness of this. The car swerves.

The man laughs. "You're a piece of shit," he says. "Just like me." He laughs again and mostly pulls your dress back up.

We are on the edge of the city now, and he orders you to stop in a half-vacant industrial park. We pull up next to the railroad tracks that parallel the street. There are no cars coming. On the other side of the tracks, housing developments begin and follow one another for miles. We are a few blocks from the bus station. Out here, all is quiet, save for the mechanized dinging when he opens the door. The dome light comes on, and before he leaves, he reaches up and shuts it off.

I watch him climb over the tracks behind the car, and then he is gone from sight. We are both breathing again, but everything else is different. I say, "We're okay," because

I want to fill the silence. Because I'm too ashamed to make this into a question.

* * *

In this version of the story, we are in a tour group together in Mammoth Cave. Our ranger-guide keeps disappearing and reappearing to show us the sights: Fat Man's Misery, the Bottomless Pit, the Giant's Coffin, and the Methodist Church.

It's cool, but not as damp as you might think. Instead of the traditional incandescent spotlights, they've put colored filters over them, as though the stalagmites are performing rock stars. The cavern is filled with red, blue, and green light that makes it nearly impossible to interpret your facial expressions.

When we reach the point in the tour where the ranger turns out the lights, we are next to each other. "Let's rewind time," he says, "and experience the darkness that Stephen Bishop, the cave's first explorer, had to overcome."

The lights go off. A young family in front of us shrieks with delight, and in the darkness, I imagine them clinging to one another. On impulse, I reach for your hand, and even though it's dark, I somehow find it on the first try.

* * *

After the man leaves the car, we switch places. You are understandably rattled, but you refuse to call the cops. I drive us past the same convenience store we stopped at earlier. It remains a glowing beacon, but it's now surrounded by loose yellow tape and a fleet of police cars, their lights irradiating the darkness. We realize what has happened, and I slow down, but you say, "Keep driving. Please." I reach down and discover our cappuccino has grown cold in the console between us, and so I roll down the window and throw it out, cup and all.

"Don't you think it's odd," you finally say, "that God would bring him into our lives?" To me, this doesn't seem to be the problem, and I say so.

"I mean," you continue, "who knows what I would have done with you tonight if that man hadn't—"

After a moment's silence, I offer, "Intervened?"

"Yeah."

The fact we have somehow been spared is not easy to accept. Our church has prepared us for outlandish and horrific instances of violence. It has prepared us for martyrdom. We have read *Guideposts* and know of sinners robbing houses only to be won over by the gentle compassion of the resident Christians. We have known that guns exist and that sometimes people wield them, even if mostly in farfetched hypotheticals meant to solidify our ethical worldview.

And we have this other problem: how to admit where we've been and what we were planning on doing. I don't know when the moment of complicity happens, but we are resolute, even now. We knew we wouldn't talk about it.

* * *

In this version of the story, I am a congregant at a church in Florida, and you have come down to our river to be baptized. You sit on a submerged bucket and wait patiently while the pastor delivers his message. "And they will know you are Christians by your love," he says, because we are an accepting lot and have ignored your tattoos and piercings, your somber demeanor and black clothes. We are adept at recognizing ourselves in other incarnations.

The sacrament continues. The congregation watches from the near shore and holds umbrellas to shield themselves from relentless sun. I am not with them. I wait downstream, hip-deep in brown water, and keep a large alligator at bay with a tree limb. As the pastor drones on, I push the alligator's snout so the events can proceed without interruption, without this unwelcome visitor.

The pastor prays to the heavens without acknowledging me, and then in an instant when my gaze is turned, he tips you back and you are baptized.

Afterward, you hug the elders and stand to one side, your hair tangled and dripping. The light shines on you, and you wipe your face in a way that makes you look like you are praying, giving thanks, I imagine, for the protection you've been afforded.

*　*　*

The night of the soiree, we return to the church and lie on storm grating at the edge of the retention pond, a stone's throw from a set of enormous crosses. The only sound is traffic on the nearby interstate, a low swooshing punctuated by jake braking. It seems like a hundred minutes pass this way. The east grows pregnant with dawn. I notice you shivering, so I offer you my tweed jacket, which you shoulder reluctantly. Finally, I offer to pray together, and we pretend to. I say the Lord's Prayer silently, because I can't search for other words.

I don't know if you prayed or what you found in those moments.

At last, I feel I must, and so I apologize. I say, "I'm so sorry," and as I say it, I realize it refers to both a dozen things and nothing at all.

You say, "Me too."

These are the last things we will say to each other. The group spills out from the front of the church where they have been inside playing games and making joyful noises unto the Lord. Everyone is waiting on breakfast and has come outside to see the sun rise. When they find us, they ask what we've been doing and I say, "Talking."

You say, "Praying and talking."

As activities, these are nearly irreproachable. I imagine it doesn't sit well with your boyfriend, but he says nothing as we rejoin the group.

* * *

In this version of the story, we enroll in a community pottery class somewhere in the mountains. The air is dry and pure, and class coincides with the golden hour—when the earth tips to just the right angle, the sun spills in the studio windows, and the balance between shadow and light becomes perfect.

We sit on opposite sides of the room and watch each other work. You have a way with the clay, with your hands. I imagine you were a baker in a previous life. The instructor tells us, "Trapped air can cause clay to explode," and to illustrate the importance of this, he stabs his demonstration piece repeatedly. More often, he says, "Find the center."

You wear a man's broadcloth shirt with the sleeves rolled up. Hair sometimes falls in your eyes, but you stay with it. You produce ashtrays and mugs, flowerpots and animals, but when your turn comes to bake it in the kiln, you balk. "It's not ready yet," you say. "The clay is too thick." You retreat to your wheel and poke at the project with a pencil eraser.

One week, I follow you to your station. I don't reach you in time to save your last project, a bowl you re-wet and ball up.

I say, "May I?" and together we begin sculpting.

The instructor sees this was inevitable and comes by to offer counsel. He puts an arm around each of us and says, "Find the center."

We do. The sunlight bakes us orange and then wanes, and the face that takes shape beneath us is what Cleopatra might have looked like after a disastrous prom night.

* * *

The other day, I saw you from a distance, or I thought I did. You walked hurriedly, head down against a gray wind. You wore sunglasses, short, sensible hair and a wedding ring on your finger. You were hurrying to catch a train in the city where we now live, and you paused. I was sitting in the park with a brown bag lunch, and for a moment, you were near me. You began to pat your pockets as if you had forgotten something small but important. There was still a little distance between us, but upon failing to find whatever it was, you exhaled sharply and looked directly at me, your eyes beautiful and tired. I nearly rose to comfort you.

We could, I thought, in spite of our ghosts. We could, I thought, because of our ghosts.

Of course, it wasn't you, but for a moment it was. Always my impulse is to replace you, to relegate you to anecdote, but I never succeed, and so I find you again and again.

Ultimately, here's what is real: The alligator. The bowling alley. A mall food court in Atlanta. You. Me. The bust of Cleopatra. All that innocence and possibility. All that is and was and is never to come.

KING KARATE

A bstract

Much attention has been paid to father-son relationships in popular society. There are father-son days almost
everywhere—in the workplace, at baseball games, at amuse-
ment parks— but there are fewer father-daughter days.

In this experiment, it was the experimenter's aim to test
the limits of a father-son relationship to see if it truly is
stronger than that of a father-daughter relationship. For
this, the experimenter framed her brother for a small crime
and documented the results, but she didn't come to many
conclusions.[1]

Investigative Question, Purpose, and Hypothesis

The experimenter was not jealous of her brother, but she
didn't think it was right that he continually got away with

---

[1] *Note*: Miss Copeland, I know this is supposed to be a scientific experiment, as this paper is for the annual science fair, but as you know,
I struggled to come up with an idea. I just couldn't bring myself to
bury trash in the backyard or compare battery strengths. You suggested I could even check how many bricks my father could break given
different materials, but I figured then I'd only be making more trash
someone would eventually have to bury. I suppose if I were like the
other kids, I'd just make something up (like last year, Erica Tolbert
never found the Chinese takeout boxes she buried and faked all her
results), but I didn't want to do that. I hope you'll understand.

everything that he did,[2] and she thought her father should know the truth: that his son was the town's at-large graffiti artist, the one responsible for obscene words tagged in cursive on prominent landmarks. Her question became: what would it take to make her father see this, and even if he did, would it be enough for him to waver in his opinion of his son?

It was and remains, in the experimenter's mind, a scientific question.[3] Her hypothesis was that she believed it would take an act of God[4] or the police to make her father see his son as anything but perfect.

Introduction

For eight years, the experimenter's father, Joshua King, has run King Karate out of an old storefront in downtown Silverton, Pennsylvania. Mr. King lives above the studio with his family: the experimenter and her brother. Recently, Mr. King instituted a male-only class on homeland security with the aim of teaching men to defend their families. For this, he took out thirty-eight urinal ads across the city, believing this to be the fairest, most visible way of advertising. He told the experimenter, "Everyone has to pee. Plus, you never know who might need it. You can never be sure where threats will come from."

---

[2] Mostly, I didn't like that he snuck out at night when my father thought he was sleeping.

[3] Like I said, Miss Copeland, I could have done the trash, but it wouldn't have been half as meaningful.

[4] I'm sorry you don't believe in God, Miss Copeland. My father agrees and says what you teach us about the Big Bang is "hogwash." He says if I want an experiment to prove it, I should take apart my CD player, put it in a shopping bag and shake it up. If it comes back together, he says I can believe in the Big Bang. If it doesn't, he says I can learn something about electronic circuitry to use for next year's science fair.

However, most of the men who showed up were the types with desk jobs. At the dinner table, Mr. King referred to them as "men who need training to be men." He said he wanted to teach them how to become better fathers. "It's not that I'm a perfect father," he said, "but I definitely have something to offer them."

Some of the women of Silverton felt it wasn't right to keep women out of the class, and a few of them took to protesting across the street. They wore strange clothing and carried mugs that resembled the ones schoolchildren sometimes make in art class. After their first couple of appearances, Mr. King (hereafter referred to as Father) sent the experimenter across the street to deal with them. One of them, named Ingrid, made an impression on the experimenter. She was kind and explained the problem like this: It was okay for Father to have all-male classes, but since he received city money, he should also have all-women classes to make up for it.

It seemed fair. The town's mayor had recently started an initiative called, "Slim it down, Silverton," and had started paying for the town to exercise. Father's studio was one of the few places where the townspeople could spend their vouchers. Ingrid also explained that she didn't think it was right that Father had recently fired a woman who used to clean the studio. Her name was Charlotte, and Father didn't think she was right in the head. He worried she might steal things while she cleaned. The experimenter told Ingrid this, and Ingrid nodded.

The women returned several times, and each time, they brought larger and more alarming props of protest. First, it was a sign that said, "Karate for All." Then, they brought a papier- mâché piñata in the shape of a crown and broke it open (leaving litter on the street within a few feet of an oversized trashcan from the mayor's "Pick It Up, Pitch It In" campaign).[5] And finally, they brought a giant inflatable rat, tall enough to peek into the experimenter's bedroom window when air was circulated through it.[6]

Each time the women came, the experimenter was sent out to deal with them while her brother stayed inside and helped with Father's class. The experimenter first tried the following:

She said, "Excuse me."

The women continued to talk, so the experimenter raised her voice and tried again. "Ladies," she said more loudly than she probably should have.

The one nearest to her, Ingrid, looked over, and the experimenter imagined her karate uniform made an impression. The woman looked the experimenter's belt, and the others, drawn by her attention, fell silent as well.

"Who are you?" Ingrid asked.

"I could ask you the same thing."

The others laughed a little bit. "She's feisty," one of them said.

Ingrid held out an empty hand for the experimenter to shake. "You must be the daughter."

The experimenter didn't shake her hand, even though karate etiquette emphasized respect. The experimenter said, "I know this is a public street, but I think you should go. You're making the men nervous."

This delighted the women. "That's sweet of you to be concerned for them," Ingrid said.

---

[5] The experimenter greatly admires the mayor and all he's done for the town of Silverton.

[6] They never left it overnight, but the experimenter could hardly sleep at night after she saw it in her window that first time.

"It's hard for them to be seen coming to this class," the experimenter said. "You should go, give them privacy."

They were all quiet for a minute. Ingrid sighed and looked at the others as though she was trying to decide the experimenter's fate.

"I'm sorry," she said, "but we're not going anywhere."

Meanwhile, the experimenter's brother, Peter, was a golden child, a prince to his father's karate empire. And when the men came to class, they nodded to him as though he were a sort of prodigy. They had heard the story of a local insurance salesman who nearly qualified to get his black belt. As a final test of will, Father forced him to run five miles in the snow without shoes on and sent Peter along to keep him honest. Without being told to, Peter took off his shoes as well.

And when the man stumbled to a halt halfway through the quest, it was the experimenter's brother who helped him finish.[7]

At school, the teachers loved Peter and the experimenter. They praised their self-reliance and discipline. When others refused to work hard during gym glass, Peter and the experimenter were the ones who raced scooters and scaled the peg board. Peter even set a new school record for hanging from the aluminum pull-up bar near the locker rooms.[8]

---

[7] You should have seen his feet, Miss Copeland. I did, because we still share a room together. They looked like bright purple balloons and they took half the night to thaw. I stayed up with him and sang camp songs. To Father's credit, he never knew. He sent Peter out in a pair of snow boots and a parka.

[8] You may remember this. Coach Fielder was thrilled and wrote notes all day excusing Peter from class. He raved about the performance, since it somehow reinforced his belief that the rest of his students were lazy scoundrels. "And to think," he said, "my other students can't even do one pull-up." When I stopped by, I wanted to tell him about what we went through at home, but I couldn't bring myself to do it. Father

The experimenter was, of course, a strong student in her own right, but she could never quite compete with these tales. She was more obedient, though, and while Peter was the one who received his black belt at age twelve, he was tough to keep under control. In the days after the rat incident, when the experimenter couldn't sleep, she was startled to realize that Peter was, and had been, sneaking away every night after Father went to bed.[9] The experimenter thought it was a bit like a movie, the way her brother would tiptoe to the window and crawl down the fire escape. She watched him from across the room, and after a while, she started following him.

The experimenter wasn't sure what would happen. The first night, she followed him to Megan Moore's house, and a few nights later, to Brenda Riggle's house. Both nights, just as the experimenter had nearly given up on him coming back out to the street, he emerged with the girl in hand and walked her toward different edges of town. One night, they climbed the water tower. The experimenter couldn't get close enough to hear or see what happened, but the night they went out on the old railroad trestle,[10] she was able to squat

---

always tells us it is best not to talk about the karate process with those who haven't been through it, since his studio "isn't the boys and girls club."

[9] As you know from parent-teacher conferences, our mother doesn't live with us anymore.

[10] Just so you know, Miss Copeland, everyone knows you and your teacher friends went out there last summer to drink jug wine and jump off the bridge. Our informant is good; she even got close enough to hear the false bravado of everyone, like when Mr. Spears said, "If only our students could see us now!" It was, in the informant's opinion, sort of sad. And the informant also saw how scared you were when Mr. Spears suggested jumping into the river below, and how you stepped back from the edge at the last minute and listened to him call you a "commie chicken."

in the low bushes near enough to the edge of the tracks to see her brother walk out to the first maintenance platform.

He asked Brenda Riggle, "What shall I paint for you?"

His voice was formal and sincere. He shook a can of paint and climbed under the railing of the trestle. When Brenda spoke, the experimenter could tell she was delighted by Peter's stupid risk. "Oh, I don't know," she said. "What can you paint?"

"Anything you want," he said. He swung upside down and dangled from the edge of the platform.

"How about a phoenix?" she said.[11]

"I don't know," Peter said. "How about a snowman?"

"I thought you could paint anything," she said.[12]

"Sure, I can, but I have to consider my trademarks."

For a while, they were silent, except for the soft sound of air escaping Peter's aerosol paint can. Every so often, he'd shake the can, and the clatter of the marble inside echoed through the ravine. The moon was full that night, and the experimenter had little trouble making out what was happening.

"What if a train comes?" Brenda asked.

"They never do."

"Still, though. I'd be afraid to run with such big cracks between the ties. Just talking about it, I'm already having visions of dismemberment."

When they finished, the experimenter stayed in the bushes as they walked back toward the town. She crawled out on the trestle and looked over the edge. It was a difficult feat to

---

[11] Is this the sort of things girls are supposed to want, Miss Copeland? Does Mr. Spears take stupid risks just to impress you? Do you make small, strange requests so that he feels strong and able to provide for you?

[12] Oh, Brenda.

accomplish, but when she did, she realized her brother must be the one responsible for the wave of graffiti all over town, for there, next to a drawing of a butterfly, was the perfect cursive handwriting that had made recent appearances all over town. What was written was a word too vulgar for the experimenter to include here in this paper, and even though she didn't need to, she reached out and touched the cold metal and felt the paint, fresh and wet beneath her fingertips.

Materials & Method

It took a while for the experimenter to devise an appropriate experiment for her original problem. She knew there were many ways to deal with what she had seen on the train trestle, and before trying anything else, she tried talking with Peter.

She met him on the fire escape, where they'd talked for years. Peter was doing wall sits against the side of the building. The experimenter joined him. They talked first about their father's new class and the protestors who had been building like an ice jam outside their front windows.

The experimenter said, "I'm sure you noticed them."

"Yeah, but I wouldn't worry too much."

"Why not?"

"Well, they're just mad because they don't understand. Dad's trying to help his students become better men, and as soon as that happens, everyone benefits. For starters, everyone's safer."

"Why can't women defend themselves?" Peter thought about it.

The experimenter asked, "Why do boys think they have to fight the world?"[13] And Peter laughed.

---

[13] Miss Copeland, I know I might be wrong, but you told us that if we ask good enough questions, science can help us answer them.

Finally, she said, "I thought you didn't like the class." It was true; he'd said as much after some of the early classes.

"It's not perfect, but it's good for some of the men," he said.

The experimenter's legs were beginning to shake. She readjusted her feet.

Peter noticed. He said, "Take your mind off it. Then you won't have to do that."

She did her best to comply, but even still she had to readjust several more times before Peter was done with his sit. The experimenter wanted to ask about Peter's artwork on the trestle, but she couldn't bring herself to do so.

Materials list for the final experiment:

- A 35-foot length of thick nylon rope
- 2 cans of spray paint, one green and one black
- 1 alligator mask and a change of dark clothing
- 1 copy of *Write the Right Way*, a cursive style guide (as seen previously in the experimenter's brother's backpack)
- 1 headlamp with extra batteries
- 3 maximum-strength, Knock Me Out Cold & Sinus tablets,[14] 500 mg. each; ground to a powder
- 1 large trash bag

Method:

1) In preparing the evening meal, the experimenter, served Father three of the KMO tablets in his mashed potatoes.

---

[14] This a British cold medicine to which Father is partial. Its a.m. equivalent is called, I kid you not, Miss Copeland, "Knock Me Up Cold & Sinus" and contains caffeine to help the British patient wake up in the morning despite their cold.

2) The experimenter waited patiently for Peter to leave their shared bedroom and for Father to begin snoring.

3) Under the cover of darkness, the experimenter climbed to the roof of King Karate and tied the thirty-five foot rope to a stove vent.

4) The experimenter then rappelled[15] feet from the ledge to where the red, white, and blue "King Karate" sign graced the middle of the storefront.

5) The words "down with tyranny" were then spray-painted over the sign, the cursive script consistent with Peter's style guide (and with his previous handiwork). Green paint was used first, and then it was covered in black, because the experimenter was worried it wouldn't be visible.

6) Returning to solid ground, the experimenter bagged up the other materials and walked them several blocks to one of the mayor's more secluded oversized trashcans.

7) The experimenter returned to her room before Peter and slept until morning.[16]

Results

The experiment was not discovered immediately the next morning. At breakfast, Father discussed his class with Peter, while Peter, bored, looked repeatedly out the window. Peter only ate two pieces of freedom toast,[17] which was strange

---

[15] Miss Copeland, you were the one that suggested I start watching the *Science & Survival Network*.

[16] All of this may not seem like much of an experiment, but don't you ever get sick of studying results that someone or something else came up with? Don't you ever dream of being the catalyst in a chemical reaction?

[17] Our father refuses to let us call it French toast.

since they are his favorite breakfast food. Meanwhile, Father ate his usual six. The experimenter, too nervous to eat, had only half of one.[18]

Father made two declarations and one announcement during the meal. He said, "I slept like a log" and "This milk has turned." He put down his fork down for the announcement. He said, "The mayor is coming to class tonight."

Peter looked unimpressed. He said, "He needs help being a man?"

I thought Father would be mad, but he laughed. "No, nothing like that," he said. "I think he's coming to straighten out that protestor thing."

Naturally, this made the experimenter quite nervous.[19]

When Peter and the experimenter left for school, the walk to school took eleven minutes. Peter did not look back at the studio even once, which led the experimenter to believe he hadn't seen the sign. Much later, she realized his lack of looking back meant he'd seen it on his way back the night before.

But in that moment, she didn't know.

He said, "I heard you're running for class president."

The experimenter must have nodded, because he continued, "If you give me some of your campaign signs, I'll hang them up in the boys' restrooms."

---

[18] I was having trouble with my computer, so I don't have the tables section ready. Someday, you'll be able to see a bar graph of this. It's on my computer somewhere. It clearly shows the difference in data. I think you'll like it.

[19] I really like Mayor Ramsey. We took time off from the Revolutionary War to talk about it in Mr. Dunn's social studies class, and we all agree he's done a wonderful job with our town. He's so honest and motivated. He's the one who's inspired me to run for class president.

She laughed, but she could hardly look at him. In between glances over at him, the experimenter stared at the sidewalk in front of her feet.

Peter said, "Keep your head up, kiddo." And that was the last of the conversation.

At school, the day passed slowly for the experimenter. She had expected this, and she was nervous throughout the day. So nervous that she broke two beakers in Miss Copeland's science class. The first was full of boiling water and was an accident,[20] but the second was on purpose. It was empty. The experimenter made sure.[21] She wanted detention so she wouldn't have to arrive home the same time as Peter. Miss Copeland gave her detention and called the experimenter "clumsy" in front of her friends and potential constituents.

During detention, the experimenter hoped Miss Copeland would ask how her science fair project was coming along. Instead of working on homework or reading, the experimenter sat with her palms flat on the table in front of her. Occasionally, she lifted her hands and looked at the greasy spots left by her sweat. She was hoping Miss Copeland would ask if something was wrong. The experimenter felt they shared something in common, something more than the genetic similarities everyone shares, and even though she'd been obnoxious in class, she hoped Miss Copeland would still talk with her.

The experimenter did speak a little bit, but didn't say what she wanted to. She wanted to ask about Marie Curie and the other female pioneers of science. She wanted to ask how Miss Copeland had chosen to study science. Instead,

---

[20] You see, this is the truth, Miss Copeland. I wouldn't lie in a scientific paper.

[21] I'm really sorry about both beakers. I am.

she asked, "May I use the restroom?" And Miss Copeland told her she'd have to wait.[22]

The walk home from school took 27 minutes. The experimenter considered taking longer, but she didn't know where she'd go. She hypothesized there would be police cars waiting for her brother, and she would have to watch him taken away in handcuffs. The mayor might be there too. She hypothesized he'd be clapping at the arrest of the graffiti artist who had been plaguing his town.[23] He might even make a speech.

When the experimenter came to her street, however, there was nothing to be seen. There was no rat. No protestors. Only Peter up on a very long ladder repainting the studio's sign. When she got closer, she saw the paper sign on the door that read: "Sorry, tonight's classes are cancelled."

The experimenter didn't want to ask what had happened. She was pleased there were no cars or protestors or rats and didn't want to mess it up. Her original experiment was on track, so she said, "What are you doing?"

Peter looked down at her. "You should talk with Father."

"Did the mayor come?" she asked.

"Yeah, he came and went."

The experimenter's heart might have skipped a beat or two.[24] She couldn't tell if she was in trouble or not. She went

---

[22] Remember? You were grading the whole time I was there, and every time you caught me looking at you, you looked out the window or toward the clock. You kept reminding me of the time. You'd see me and say, "Only twenty-five minutes." Or, "twelve more minutes." You might understand now that those were the worst things you could have said to me.

[23] He had vowed to catch the person who was defacing Silverton landmarks, and before I knew who it was, I cheered this announcement.

[24] I know you told us this doesn't actually happen unless we have a heart condition, but that's what it felt like in my chest.

inside. Father sat with his legs crossed, in a position of quiet contemplation. She recognized it from his classes. It was the way every workout ended. She noticed his uniform was still wet with sweat.

Not wanting to interrupt him, the experimenter began to walk past, but Father called out to her. She paused at the bottom of the stairway. He spoke so quietly the experimenter had to cross the room to understand him. And when she was that close, the experimenter thought he might have been crying.

"Claire," he said. "I'm listening."

Conclusions

It was the intent of this project to test the strength of the father-son bond against the father-daughter bond, but the experimenter made a great many errors in the process of her experiment. She failed to identify all her variables, even though she believes it might have been an impossible task. She failed to do full and proper research. And she didn't have a control group.[25] Actually, she failed to control much of anything.

Therefore, the results are imperfect and incomplete. Someday, the experimenter hopes to come to fuller and more complete conclusions, but she is willing to admit that day is not today.[26]

---

[25] I'm still not sure what this is, Miss Copeland.

[26] Please don't fail me for not understanding everything, Miss Copeland. I may need your help to analyze the data I've collected. I realize that, and I'm sorry for not asking sooner. But whatever you do, please, please, please, don't fail me.

MARS RENAISSANCE: EIGHT THINGS A MAN SHOULD KNOW HOW TO DO

Listen

They are sending Lisa and me down to the capital for a statewide charity function our office doesn't care about. We've been invited during our peak season, and our boss, a not-quite-motherly figure named Gretchen, tells us someone needs to go as a show of solidarity. "It's like the golden rule," she says. "You help support other charitable causes so they will support yours."

We are seated in her office, among a menagerie of large and gaudy animal carvings. Our boss buys them from artisan guilds in developing countries. To the rest of us, they are nothing more than an expensive eyesore.

"I would go, but I'm busy," she says. She leans back against her desk and lets her hand rest on one of the giraffes. She looks at me. "And you know we can't send Edgar."

It's true. I do know Edgar can't go. Worse yet, he would drag along his wife, a drab chain-smoker who collects Coca-Cola memorabilia and talks about it.

"But why us?" we say to fill the silence.

"Relax. It should be fun. It'll be a free trip to Indianapolis. And you'll give our organization a young face."

"But you don't look a day over thirty," I say.

It's not a great joke, but she doesn't react, which is sort of maddening. "I said I'm busy," she says.

Attempts at obvious brown-nosing aside, I'm somewhat scared of Gretchen. Of her animals, her femininity, her name. It doesn't roll off anyone's tongue.

*　*　*

The event is three weeks away, but my apprehension is immediate. I've had a crush on Lisa Mayes since last Thursday, when she started working with us. We've had only limited interactions—always professional, yet quasi-intimate. Our office is a small, local chapter of a larger nonprofit. Aside from Lisa and me, we only have six employees: Leonard (an alcoholic in a bad marriage who sometimes sleeps in his office), Gretchen (the boss), Edgar, Robert (pronounced "row bear" and reiterated so often that we call him 'Silent T'), Beverly (our administrative assistant and resident cheerleader) and Bianca (a shadowy enigma of a woman who dresses darkly and pilfers poetry books from the donation piles). Desiree and Martin also used to work with us, but they were let go for simultaneous but unrelated embezzling schemes.

I believe one of them could have gotten away with it if they hadn't done it at the same time. And if Martin hadn't installed an above-ground pool in his backyard and invited us over for drinks.

The day Lisa arrives, I am immediately interested in her. It's a truism that a man within eyesight of a woman knows within fifteen seconds whether or not he'd ever sleep with her. That morning, I have to help her set up her workstation—an operation that requires much incidental leaning-over and reaching-around. I keep it professional—I'm not a creep—but the feeling that comes over me is strange.

Her hair is short and curly, and she smells good, like a flower I don't have a name for. She has an otherworldly dimension about her; she wears a long, arm-length sweater with a small, crane-shaped pin attached to the lapel.

When I notice this, I say, "Have you seen Gretchen's animals?"

"No?" she says, and I get to laugh and tell her about the boss's fair-trade zoo.

"When she interviewed me, we met for coffee around the corner. And she didn't show me her office on the tour."

It's neutral. She doesn't seem willing yet to ally herself with me over her boss. I make a small, interested noise and sneak a look at her cleavage. "Well, you should see them sometime," I say. But she won't until the following Tuesday when we're called in to discuss the charity function.

Cook

On Saturday, I go shoot guns with my buddy, Clark. He lives on some land outside the city, so we do it in his backyard. For weeks, I've been taking care of the office's recycling, and I bring it over, along with a twelve-pack of Schlitz, our preferred beer. When I arrive, I pull around back. There's no sign of Clark, save for his cooler and his gun. I go to fill the cooler before I realize it's already full of expensive German beer. I stare at it. The bottles are green, and as they lie half-suspended in the ice, their shape seems distinctly un-American. I cover them with the Schlitz.

Clark comes out of the house. Since work has been busy, I haven't seen him in a while. He's wearing a button-down shirt and a pair of striped shorts. "Where have you been?" I ask.

"Sorry, I was trying to finish the chapter of the book I'm reading."

"What's with the fancy clothes?" I ask. "You have to work today?"

"I haven't left the house. Come on, let's shoot."

He grabs the bag of recycling out of my hand and walks out to where we've set hay bales along the tree line. "This is a good batch," he calls to me. "A lot of soup cans."

"You know how it is," I say. "I work with liberals and health nuts."

I think of Lisa. I remember how I walked past the lounge earlier in the week and saw her eating soup.

Clark comes back to where I'm standing. I open a couple beers for us. "Thatta boy," he says. "We're not getting any younger."

He moves to the cooler and rummages under the Schlitz for a green bottle. He cracks it with an opener from his back pocket. He notices me watching him.

"You're up," he says and hands me his gun.

* * *

Afterward, we move inside and sit down in front of the TV. I flip to the main sports channel, but all that's on is women's basketball. I look around for another distraction. There's no mistaking that the room is cleaner than my last visit. There are vacuum lines in the carpet.

"Hiding a woman around here?" I ask.

"Nah, my allergies have been acting up," he says. "I figured it might be the dust."

I accept this. I turn back to the TV. On it, a woman makes a breakaway layup for the home team. They cut to the camera under the basket as she turns and runs back down the floor.

"You hungry?" Clark asks.

"Am," I say. Then, gesturing at the TV, I say, "That broad's sort of hot."

"Which one?" he asks.

The TV shows a guard bringing the ball up the floor. It's the same one who made the layup. I point at her. Clark nods in agreement.

"I can make some pasta al fresco," he says. "That okay?"

"Your phone broken?"

"No."

"Why don't we just order a pizza? What's your deal, man?"

He is silent for a minute. I've stopped him halfway to the kitchen. He says, "What if we're still doing this when we're forty—wrecking ourselves with fast food and ogling unattainable women on the TV because we can't love ourselves and sustain real relationships?"

I turn back to the TV and stare at the crawl on the bottom of the screen, even though I fail to absorb the words. Eventually, when I say nothing, he crosses the room and pulls a book out from under the coffee table. I read the cover aloud, *Mars Renaissance: Eight Things a Man Should Know How to Do.*

"You going gay on me?" I ask, but I note the book's name.

Converse

At work, I see little of Lisa. Gretchen has put her on a project that keeps her busy most days and out of the common areas. The two of them spend most of the morning on conference calls to India. No one explains it to me, but I figure it must be because of the time zones.

Meanwhile, I am relegated to local campaigns with Silent T. We spend time away from the office, canvassing the nearby neighborhoods for donations for our annual budget. It goes like this: We knock on a door. Occasionally, someone answers. Robert introduces himself, complete with the "silent-t" routine. We spiel. We pause meaningfully. We hand out business cards. We discourse. We ask. We ask again.

They ask: "What did you say your organization does?" We ask, "If you were to die next week, what legacy would you leave?" We badger. We ask, "If you were to die next week, how much do your children really need?" We threaten to move in on their couch. They relent. They concede. They give us a ten-dollar check, a box of old LPs, and a broken toaster.

* * *

Our office makes many phone calls. There are, in fact, more phone lines than employees.

In the afternoons, we are all supposed to call people and secure pledges. Our budget is under constant siege. In the afternoons, Beverly calls her children and walks them home from school on their cell phones. Silent T calls the home shopping network and begs whoever answers to talk dirty. Edgar calls his wife. Gretchen calls obscure countries and chases after new artisan guilds. Leonard takes a nap and calls no one. Bianca somehow has a private line.

Lisa calls businesses and philanthropists. I'm not a creep, but I listen to her calls. I listen to her voice and imagine her in my bedroom, making polite but urgent requests of me.

With Lisa, it's more than some trite man-lust. I have slept with what I think is a healthy number of women, but she persists in my mind, not because I believe she's unattainable, but because she wears full-length sweaters, and because she's in constant proximity. I don't want to conquer her. I don't want to mount her on my wall. Rather, I want to do it more than once with her.

One day, Lisa takes the afternoon off from her usual phone calls. With nothing worth listening to, I wander the building and find her in the lounge. She's drinking water out of a glass jar and rummaging through the game cabinet. She looks up when I walk in. "Want to play Scrabble?" she asks.

I nod. We play. She wins by building off my simpler words. Her best word: *supercilious.*

I look it up after I lose.

*   *   *

On the way home, I stop at a bookstore. I scour the shelves for the book Clark recommended, but it's nowhere to be found. I am about to give up when I see a man walk away from the sales counter with book-sized brown paper bag. I begin to ask, "Do you have—"

He cuts me and lifts a copy of *Mars Renaissance* from beneath the counter. He shoves it in a brown bag identical to the one the other man had. I thank and pay him.

In the privacy of my home, I examine the book. I open to the back dust jacket. The book's authors, Nigel Simmons and Colin O'Neil smile up at me. I recognize them both from adolescence. Nigel once wore a Lord Fauntleroy shirt to a junior high dance and tried to claim he found it in his parents' attic. Colin took ballet to help his athletic footwork but continued lessons after the season ended. Nigel made elaborate dishes in home economics and was suspended once for bringing cooking wine to school. Colin regularly hosted black-tie parties at his parents' remodeled Victorian. My friends and I once nearly beat up both of them during a school assembly. We were all jealous of their bevy of lady friends.

The first chapter is called, "The day I stopped hunting and learned to love myself."

I begin reading: *This is not a book about how to get laid, at least not in a classical sense. This is a book about finding a cleaner, more stylish and well-rounded version of you! This is about breaking free of cliché and overcoming the unsatisfactory and primordial patterns of lust and conquest. This book is about discovering the true power of being a male. It is a lesson in how to be a modern man.*

I flip to another page. "It's about empowerment," Colin says. "If you change yourself preemptively, women won't have that power over you."

"Mars is a beautiful planet," Nigel adds.

The eight things are listed in the table of context, first under the heading "remedial work"—cook, clean, listen—then under "survival skills"—shop, converse, seduce—and finally under "higher functions"—lead, dream.

There's a pocket guide too. It comes disguised as a Moleskine notebook.

* * *

I try talking to Clark about Lisa a week after the German beer incident. I meet him for lunch near the bank where he works. He has shaved his goatee.

"I don't know," I say. "I took home someone from the bar the other night, but I keep thinking about Lisa."

"That's how you know it's special," he says.

His salad arrives. He finishes it before the waitress brings my patty melt. When she does, I flirt with her and watch her backside all the way back to the kitchen.

Nigel and Colin are seated at the booth beside us. Nigel says, "Trade in your telescope for a microscope. Don't gaze at Venus until you've classified all that's on Mars."

"I bought the book," I say to Clark.

He quiets me and his eyes grow strange. He says, "It's a private and personal journey."

I protest. "But I recognize your change in facial hair from chapter two," I say.

Colin says, "Imperative: No goatees, no soul patches, no mustaches, and no neck beards."

"And when you shave," Nigel adds. "Use gentle strokes. It's not a race."

"Can I just ask you this?" I say to Clark. "Do you hear them too?"

"All the time," he says.

Clean

At home, they've been going through my closets. In the evenings, as I'm in the shower, Nigel peruses my work clothes. He condemns and pronounces. He relays his questions to Colin, who sits on my toilet seat and gives me advice about exfoliation and skin hydration. "What are you going to wear to the big charity event?" he asks.

"I don't know," I say. "I have a suit somewhere in my closet."

"Oh no," I hear Nigel yell. "Not this! It looks like something you picked up at Sears for a '95 fraternity formal."

"I was in elementary in '95," I say.

"So was I," he says, "but I still knew better."

On the way to work, they ride in the backseat and make fun of the men we see in passing cars. "They all look so pathetic," Nigel says. "So devoid of imagination."

"Quick! What are two great flaws of the male gender?" Colin asks.

"Lack of subtlety and lack of spontaneity," I say. It was part of the end-of-chapter quiz.

Colin reaches over the seat and shoves a CD into the stereo. Jazz begins playing.

"And why shouldn't men give in to the hunter mentality?" Nigel asks.

"It's a cliché and a trap. Women use sex to manipulate men," I say. "Let me ask you something: are you two… you know."

They look at each other. After a beat, they say, "No, of course not."

Nigel says, "We love having sex."

Colin says, "With women."

Nigel says, "Haven't we made that clear?"

Colin says, "We're trying to get you laid in a meaningful way."

Seduce

It's a week and a half before the event, and I'm not making progress with Lisa. I've given up nearly all of my fantasies of what it will be like. Beyond professional interactions, she barely registers my existence.

Nigel reassures me. "This is exactly where you want her," he says. "You want her to feel safe; she'll put up defenses if she feels a threat."

Colin says, "Avoiding tags like 'creepy' is half the battle for men. And what have we learned about tags?"

"Even if you remove them, there's always sticky residue?"

Colin starts to correct me, but Nigel stops him. "Close enough," he says. "It's just not a road you want to travel."

That afternoon, Gretchen calls me into her office without Lisa. There's a new wooden orangutan dangling from the ceiling fan. I must be staring, because Gretchen asks, "Do you like him?"

I don't. I say, "How do you know it's a boy?"

"It's easy to see from my side of the desk."

I look around the room. "What else is new?"

"I'm afraid we're not going to have the funds to send you to that charity function," she says. And for a moment, I'm relieved. Because I'm curious, I ask, "What happened to solidarity of charitable causes?"

"Oh, we're still sending Lisa," she says, "but we can't afford two hotel rooms."

"But she's so new," I say.

"And we need a fresh face."

This is the most confrontational Gretchen and I have ever been. For a fleeting moment, I get the feeling I could sweep clear her desk and send her animals into prudish migration. But Nigel speaks up.

"This isn't what we talked about," he says. He leans against the filing cabinet in the corner and pets the jointed snake that's draped over its edge.

I ask Gretchen, "What if we share a room?" She laughs at this. "I doubt that's a possibility."

* * *

Later in the hallway, I corner Bianca.

"What do you do with all those poetry books?" I ask.

"What books?"

It's a tack I'd expected. "I need them for a project I'm working on," I say.

Reluctantly, she leads me back to her office. Behind her printer—behind her printer!— there's a stack of slim poetry volumes. I choose one called *Approximate Center* and read at random. The first three lines mention, in order: desire, artichoke hearts, callouses, and ennui. I take it from her.

"Thank you," I say. "This should be perfect."

What I'm hoping for are sound bites, phrases I can internalize and adapt for my own purposes. Nigel has suggested this.

"You want to join the conversation," he says.

Lisa likes poetry, or at least I think she does. She went to school for literature and has ended up working at our humble nonprofit due to her highly developed sense of sympathy and a nonexistent job market. At least that's how I imagine it happening. I can't imagine someone like her failing at much of anything.

Colin tells me this is a dangerous sort of female objectification. He tells me I need to stop imagining that attractive or talented women are any closer to perfect than I am.

Shop
I talk with Clark the following weekend. We go shopping together, as male friends are prone to do.

In the car, I thumb through chapter four, which covers shopping. "What do you make of all this?"

"What are you doing?"

"What?"

"You can't read the book during a live scenario."

"It's not a live scenario." I feel obligated to point this out. "We're not shopping yet."

Clark pauses and honks at a car stopped ahead of us. "It's like listening to the CD of a band you're about to see in concert. It's decidedly uncool."

This is more the old Clark. I'm happy for a moment, until Colin chimes in from the backseat. "That doesn't sound like very effective communication," he says.

"I feel bullied right now," I say and Clark nods.

"That's more like it," Colin says. "Now you're communicating."

At the sporting goods store, we split up, but after ten minutes, we return to the front. I ask Clark what's wrong, and he tells me about a painting he saw above the urinal of a man leaving his gun and going to the restroom while a herd of deer moved by. And I, in turn, tell him about the man who tried to help me, a man who blew his nose into a handkerchief while assisting me, a gross misrepresentation of the male gender.

We don't know what to say to each other for a moment.

"So, you want to go shoot soup cans?" I ask.

But he doesn't. Instead, he says, "I don't know if we should see each other for a while." He says, "I need some time to work alone." He says, "I'm nearly finished with the book."

"Oh," I say.

* * *

At work, the budget is growing thin everywhere. There are no longer paper towels in the restroom, and the air-conditioning only runs until noon. We're a few days from the charity function. Gretchen has decided to cut down on the number of phone lines, so now instead of our old scenario—many lines, few voices—we're now forced to wait on each other to make calls.

It's highly inefficient, especially as it leads to awkward eavesdropping situations. I'm especially embarrassed to hear Edgar on the phone with Mrs. Coca-Cola. Every day at two she calls to recount her online auction victories from the previous day. It's painful, and yet I tune in like it's a radio broadcast.

On the Monday before the event, Lisa wanders by while I'm eating lunch. Since I've started cooking, I brownbag my lunches and am therefore more of a presence during the downtime. It's taught me a lot. Among other things, I've watched Bianca at work with the donation piles to where she now steals and recommends books to me, which I read and then put back on the bottom of the pile. It seems, to me, like a beautiful cycle. And Leonard, I sometimes see wandering the halls like a phantom. Even with the new phone system, I still am unsure what he does for us.

But I haven't seen much of Lisa, so I call out to her.

"Lisa," I say, and surprisingly she returns to the doorway. I look at her in a way I haven't before. Her eyes are red and puffy, as though she hasn't been sleeping, and there's a small stain on the cuff of her otherwise pristine sweater. I don't feel like I have permission to ask anything chummy like, "Hey, how you been?" or say anything corny like, "Long time, no see." Those things don't mean anything anyway, but it's what I would have tried before.

Instead, I ask, "Do you want any soup?" It's what I've brought for lunch, and I remember her fondness for it.

She smiles. "No, that's okay."

"Are you sure? It's married soup. I made it myself."

Now she's laughing. "What did you call it?"

"Married soup. Most people call it wedding soup, but that's a mistranslation of the original Italian."

"You know Italian?" she asks.

She seems impressed, but I have to admit that I don't. I ask her what she's up to. She tells me she's waiting on a phone call from an important contact and doesn't know what to do with herself, so I offer to play in a game of checkers. There's always been a chess set on Robert's desk, and I retrieve it.

"Isn't that a chess set?" she asks.

"Sure," I say, "but I don't know how to play that. We'll just use the colors like regular pieces, and when someone reaches the end, we'll put Scotch tape on the top of the piece like a crown."

And so we do, except the scotch tape ends up reminding us of the tags on Hershey kisses.

And the Hershey kisses make her think of her grandfather, who lived alone until she moved north a couple months ago to look after him.

"I had no idea," I say, but then the phone rings, and Lisa leaps up to answer it.

I resist the urge to listen in on her call. Instead, I look down at the board to where I am being overrun by her pieces.

Lead

When I get home, I open the book. Colin and Nigel have nothing to offer me. I call Clark and get a recording that tells me he's out of town on a spiritual journey. I call his folks for confirmation, and they tell me he's preparing himself for life as a monk.

"Figuratively, you mean," I say.

"No," his dad says. "We couldn't be prouder of him."

Clark's family has always been religious, but I would have thought this would be a surprise.

Finally, I call Lisa. I've had her number for weeks—having stolen it from the directory at work—but it's only now that it doesn't feel creepy.

She answers on the third ring, and I identify myself.

"Hey," she says, "sorry we didn't get to finish our game."

"It was pretty much over," I say. I ask her how her big call went and she tells me about her failure, something I could have guessed. "Budgets are tight everywhere right now," I say.

"I know," she says. "Speaking of," she begins, and then proceeds to invite me to the capital.

* * *

For a moment while I'm packing, I consider not taking the book. After all, it doesn't seem necessary. I've accomplished most of what I set out to do, and yet, I can't bring myself to leave it behind. It seems like a conundrum of the self-help genre: now that it's shown me my flaws, I can't live without it.

In the end, we take her car, even though I clean mine out just in case. On the drive down, we make casual conversation. I find out she's from Tennessee, and momentarily it reminds of that one pick-up line, but I don't say it. The old me would have, but the new me can see Nigel and Colin in the rearview mirror.

At the hotel, we park and split up. We have a while before the event, and I don't want to jinx anything. I tell her I've forgotten my cummerbund—Nigel's suggestion—and need to go find one at a men's store.

I walk the streets with Nigel and Colin rehearsing my lines for the evening. "Of course you should compliment her," Nigel says, "but don't make it anything too obvious. You know, eyes, dress, smile, so forth."

"And don't use *stunning, radiant,* or *smoking,*" Colin adds. "Those are in the trash dump of popular culture."

Nigel says, "Just be your new, better self, and you'll be fine."

"Got it," I say. "And what about the poetry?"

"You'll know if and when the time is right," Colin says. "And speaking of, don't eat too much at dinner."

For an hour or so we strategize, but when I get back to the hotel, I am confronted by the reality of my situation: this is not a black tie affair, but given my other wardrobe choices—a pair of jeans and a t-shirt or the white shirt without the jacket—I choose to endure my mistake as gracefully as I can manage.

Determined to be a gentleman, I change in the first-floor restroom. And when we reconvene in the lobby, Lisa doesn't comment on my attire, so I do. "I'm sorry," I say. "I just assumed this was black tie."

She doesn't apologize for failing to warn me. "You'll be all right," she says.

The event's held in the Azalea, Magnolia, and Robert E. Lee conference rooms. The hotel is a southern chain, and while they've slid aside the walls for us, the tracks on the ceiling reveal where the separations once were.

We find our table. They seat us with Marilynn and Leon, a couple who work for a foundation that brings art to nursing homes, and with Laura and Kristin, retired educators who recruit and train ex-marines to work in elementary schools.

We exchange perfunctory greetings. It's nothing like Gretchen promised it would be. And during dinner, everyone talks about themselves. There's no sharing of ideas or sense of community. Leon says, "If you're going to die somewhere, there should be something better than a painting of a glowing cottage on the wall." And then, as though she thinks she's responding, Laura adds, "You know, there's a real alarming lack of male role models in primary schools."

It's a wearying dinner. Lisa talks, but I don't listen. And when my entrée arrives, it's vegetarian, even though I didn't ask for it.

"This is it?" I ask Lisa.

"Everything's vegetarian unless you requested otherwise.

I don't want to admit this is what I care about. "I just meant," I say, "that it seems sort of paltry for such a nice hotel. I was expecting more."

I thought I was whispering this, but around the table everyone has ceased talking and has quieted the sound of their silverware. I'm annoyed now. I look down at my plate. I say, "And what is this garnish? Parsley? Is this 1995?"

I look across the table in time to catch Leon and Marilynn whispering among themselves.

I think they're talking about me until they gesture toward the near wall where a drawing of a lighthouse hangs. Meanwhile, Lisa has resumed talking with Laura and Kristin. I catch her saying something about the bravery of servicemen both at home and abroad.

I interrupt. I ask, "Do you call yourselves recruiters then?"

Lisa and Laura look at each other. "Well," Laura says, "we're recruiters *and* trainers."

And I say, "Don't you think it's ironic that you're recruiting them for more service? Poor men. I mean, do you give out free hackie sacks and backpacks and tell them what they'll be doing will be appreciated?" I try to smile, but all of this has come out more cruelly than I meant it, and immediately, I want to take it back.

What's worse though: they ignore me and resume their conversation. Even Lisa won't look at me. I try to think of what Nigel and Colin would have me do, but I can't. Instead, I finish off both of our table's bread baskets and an extra dessert before I stand up. I get Lisa's attention and tell her I'm going for fresh air. I try to be polite. I say, "I'm sorry. That really filled me up."

She looks perplexed. She says, "Go for it," and resumes her conversation with the recruiters.

Dream

On my walk, I begin to face difficult facts, specifically the fact that I am a dreadful bore. Lisa doesn't care about how exquisite the food is, or isn't, or what I've done. She doesn't care that much about my renaissance. I realize how I've turned this is into a game for myself—something only marginally different from the sort of hunting-and-fishing, divide-and-conquer of all my previous strategies.

I wander over to the river, where couples promenade on a waterside trail.

I sit on the edge of a flower planter. Nearby, a man whispers in his date's ear. I can't hear him, but the woman laughs loudly. She says, "I never would have even thought of that!" I sit for a bit longer, and when they stand up, I see she is wearing his suit jacket.

When they pass by me, he says, "Sharp tux, friend," and she laughs and pokes him in the ribs.

Back at the hotel, I avoid the ballrooms and head upstairs. I stop at our floor's amenities closet and fill the front of my shirt with ice. I hurry to the room and dump the ice on the floor near the door. I lose the tux in favor of an old t-shirt.

Colin says, "You've given up."

Nigel looks over my t-shirt. He says, "I could have sworn we gave that away."

"I hid it," I say.

Colin says, "So, what are we going to do now?"

I don't answer. I grab the ice bucket and position it at the end of one of the beds. I go back to the entryway and sit down next to the ice. And to their horror, I begin throwing it across the room at the ice bucket. It's something I used to do when I was young and again when Clark and I stayed in hotels on road trips. And as I do it, I begin to miss Clark.

This is, of course, where Lisa finds me. She doesn't knock, and instead I hear the key card sliding into the lock, and I barely have time to get out of the way of the door. She's carrying her shoes in her hands and looks exhausted.

"You were right to leave," she says, without preface. "Nothing happened except they brought out a speaker and this pretentious jazz—"

She pauses and looks down. Beneath her the carpet is wet from the melting ice. In that moment, I'm afraid of what she'll say. My fingers are cold, and the door remains open behind her. Briefly, I imagine barreling past her and into the night. But instead, she smiles at me in a way I could have never hoped for.

I explain. I say, "I used to do this game on family vacations. My parents weren't much for TV, so we made up whatever games we could."

She's laughing now. She lets the door close and slides down beside me. She looks in front of us toward the bucket, then over to our right at the bathroom. She says, "You ever throw at the toilet?"

I go for more ice while she changes. And we throw for a while, listening to the satisfying splash when we make it and the equally satisfying clank of ice on tile when we miss. We don't talk, lest we spoil the acoustics.

As we run out of ice, I take a piece of ice from the bucket and run it down her neck. She laughs and shrugs me off. "Knock it off, punk," she says. And I do.

She says, "That reminds me. You're never going to believe what I found in the closet." As I wait, she crosses the room and removes *Mars Renaissance* from her suitcase. "Someone left it in the top of the closet underneath the extra pillows."

"What were you doing in the top of the closet?"

"Rummaging." She smiles. "It's something I always do when I stay in hotels. You wouldn't believe what people leave behind."

In her hands, the book looks gaudy and inorganic. She holds it out to me, and I take it. I manage to laugh as I look over the cover. I open the dust jacket to Colin and Nigel. They look up at me accusingly.

Nigel says, "She feels threatened by your ambition."

Colin says, "There'll be other women, but men need to stay united."

I look up at Lisa. She's laughing. She says, "Isn't it ridiculous?"

Colin says, "Is it?"

And I have to agree that, yes, it is ridiculous, and briefly, as I close the book and cross the wet carpet to take her in my arms, I think of Clark in his new monastic existence, and my thoughts are taken to a dry brown mountainside, where it's sunset and all around me, brothers chant perfect nonsense into the dying twilight, a higher place which I recognize but do not know how to reach.

PAPER ROUTE

We started the paper route in the summer, when it seemed like a good idea. We were short on cash, and we began the route as a lark, a semi-ironic way of paying the bills. "I always wanted a paper route when I was a kid," I told her, "but my parents wouldn't let me do it." I was working then as a steam cleaner, she as a hostess at a neighborhood Italian restaurant. She'd come home smelling of garlic and cooked pasta. I would return stinking of extraction detergent and stain remover. "Jobs that stink, stink," my father had once warned me. I tried not to think of this.

Our schedules mostly missed each other. I slept in the late afternoons and evenings, she in the mornings. But we had Sundays and we had the nights, and we used them both.

It exhausted us.

We lived then near the valley, not far from the Jennings Freeway, where rent was cheap and gentrification had sputtered out far north of us. The pollution was not insubstantial, the nearby foundry's eternal flame visible from our bedroom window, its soot gritty on the sill. In a former life, our apartment had been a small church of undetermined denomination. Sometimes, on Sunday mornings, we'd wake to the sound of shuffling feet on the porch and find hopeful parishioners, dressed in Sunday finery, milling around our doorstep, puzzled or incredulous looks on their faces. Most apologized and told us that it had been their church years ago, that they'd been "away" and were hoping to visit. Whether 'away' meant from the city or from the faith we didn't ask. One intrepid asked for a tour, even though we were both still in our bedclothes, and we were so caught off guard that we acquiesced. On the tour, we didn't talk much, allowing him to wander our apartment in silence. Just in front of our toaster oven, he paused. "This is where I accepted Jesus," he said. "This used to be a Sunday school room."

After he left, she said, "Who are these people and where have they been?"

I shrugged and said I didn't know. We had both grown up in versions of the church, but I hadn't been in years and, especially with our current schedules, couldn't fathom the sacrifice of time and earnings that going would represent.

Our living room was the old sanctuary, small and octagonal, its ceiling vaulted. Near the peak, there was a circular window. The front doors were French and opened to the porch. The hardwood floors were painted white, and the lower windows were rimmed in stained glass.

What else could we do? We joked about it: our house as a church, our relationship as religion. Of course, this was probably a mistake.

* * *

Our first night on the paper route, it was balmy. June. We took my car, an old VW. The papers arrived to us on the porch; we heard the thud but didn't look out, not wanting to ruin the magic trick. We didn't want to know how they arrived, or by whom. We had stayed up late, waiting. We were nearly drunk with anticipation.

We stumbled out into the muggy morning. Low clouds bruised the sky, purple with reflected light. I called it morning. "It's night," she said, but without malice. We piled the papers into the back of my car ceremoniously, as though packing for a road trip.

"We have everything?" I asked.

"Do we need beers?"

It was a leading question, so I said we did.

And so it began. The darkness was ours, and we claimed it in blocks, tracing our progress on the map. Time and distance suspended, we orbited the fire station, our sun. We took turns delivering the papers, lobbing them toward doorways, challenging one another with outlandish, over-the-rose-bush, off-the-porch-rail shots. The car idled, unoccupied. We both smelled of exhaust. On Maplehurst, she nearly ran over my foot as she tried to drive off when I reached for the door. On 28th, a light popped on when—testing my submarine delivery—I clocked some sort of porch sculpture that rattled like a pie plate when it fell.

"Good throw," she said when I climbed back in.

With the papers gone, we went home and collapsed into bed, our breath rising and falling in unison.

* * *

The next day, I had trouble concentrating at work. I was running the big steam cleaner and working alone. The house I was cleaning was quiet; a couple—much like ourselves, I imagined—had ordered the full treatment, which meant carpet, upholstery and drapes. The occupants were on vacation. Everything was rich and heavy, and the cleaning was slow-going. In the humidity, without the ability to air things out, I imagined the rooms might take days to dry.

It was an unusual situation. Normally, the homeowners were there from the beginning and watched warily as you lugged your equipment into the house. And before taking any contract, our service encouraged but didn't mandate a walk-thru, in which the customer showed you what they worried about and what they expected. It was supposed to help set both parties at ease, assure the customers that they had some control of the operation. And from there, it was common to feel them hovering in a nearby room, listening for ominous sounds—breaking vases, steamer-furniture collisions, priceless items rattling in the steamer's tank. Once, when cleaning some newlyweds' house, I sucked up something that, when it clanked inside the cleaner, brought the husband in from his home office.

"What was that?" he asked.

I was new and scared. I admitted I didn't know.

"Well, aren't you going to look?"

His anger made him attractive, and it was then that I noticed he wasn't wearing a wedding ring. We found it in the tank, among the dirty suds.

"I was fiddling with it," he said. "It's so new." I caught him looking at my finger. "I don't suppose you'd understand that yet."

I nodded because he was right: I didn't know how it was.

Most calls weren't that remarkable, but overall, I found the job agreeable. I'd always had an affinity with the kind of small machines the average person rents but doesn't own—power washers, woodchippers, lawn aerators—something about their nature: a combination of utilitarianism and exoticism. No one expects to own that sort of powerful strangeness.

During a smoke break, I called Aubrey. She was at home, napping before work. I woke her up.

"Come on over," I said, looking through the porch window at the living room couch. "We'll have a party."

She was reluctant.

"It's all right," I said. "We won't get caught. I'll clean up afterward."

She came over but probably shouldn't have. The couple had pets, and even though I'd been cleaning it didn't prevent her from sneezing upon arrival. I apologized profusely, tried to make things right by offering her Cherry Coke from the refrigerator. It was her favorite soft drink.

"I think," she said, in between sneezes, "I'd better go."

It felt like our first failure as a couple, and after she left, the house felt much lonelier. That night, on the route, we were quiet. I'd just woken up. She'd closed at the restaurant.

We worked quickly, and as we did, we grew more talkative, felt a sense of accomplishment. There was something satisfying in the shrinking stacks in the backseat. I drove faster. She worked ahead, folding the papers, sliding them into their weatherproof bags, and marking off streets we'd completed.

She was becoming efficient. It was arousing. When we got home, we made love in the old sanctuary.

A few nights later, we stole the inserts out of the papers, all the advertisements we knew no one would miss, the ones for vinyl siding and term life insurance. We stopped near the end of our route and piled them in the middle of the street. And when we lit the fire, their glossy pages burned green and blue. We stood back and watched. The fire grew high enough that I was worried about the cops coming by, but they never came by, and we abandoned it long before it burnt itself out.

* * *

Meanwhile, my job as a steam cleaner was dissolving. Some nights after the paper route, I would crawl into bed with the intention to sleep only a couple hours, but when I woke up, I'd find the sun shining strong and disorienting through the stained glass, and I'd have to rush out the door without saying anything to Aubrey. I was late several times. My boss was a Christian and viewed me as a pitiable cause. He forgave my tardiness. To compensate and win back his favor, I worked longer hours and took extra assignments in distant suburbs.

Aubrey followed my lead. In my increasing absence, she too took on additional responsibility. The restaurant was expanding its lunch menu, pushing for a corner on the area market. And it was working. Some nights, she'd complain about how there was no longer a lull between meals. "Who eats lunch at 3 o'clock?" she'd complain. And I would listen, sympathizing.

"Freaks," I joked. "Ones with weird schedules."

But the money was nice. We bought things, began home improvement projects. Aubrey had always been an adopter of things, and our house was already filled with orphaned plants and rejected furniture, but now she supplemented her previous finds with thrift-store tapestries and small table sculptures. In our bedroom—"the fellowship hall," we called it—she placed a large candelabrum she'd found on the curb one night. On our porch, she added a doormat that read: "#blessed."

"Do you think it's too much?" she asked.

I nodded, but said, "I love it. We should wear choir robes around the house."

Our landlord was thinking of selling. In our bliss, we talked of buying, even though we knew it was beyond us.

"Haven't you always dreamed of owning a house of worship?" I asked. "We could get it for a song."

"You're becoming your father," she said but hugged me.

* * *

My father believed property to be the only true frontier for investment. It was honest, he said. If a man could save for, then buy and improve upon something, only then was he entitled to the profits. He'd been hinting at this for some time—talking of my brother's *house*, my brother's *land*, my brother's *maturity*.

But I didn't want the house to satisfy my father; I wanted it for us. It was our first place together, and we'd found it after months of fruitless searching. And yet now, neither of us spent much time in it. One night, feeling her absence, I went to her restaurant, still dressed in my Steam Brothers uniform. She met me at the door.

"Welcome to Allegro's," she said, smiling.

"You seem to be performing your job well," I said.

I leaned in for a kiss. She turned her head. "I'm going to be late tonight," she said.

I felt the draft of the door behind me as a couple came in, speaking loudly. "I gave up chocolate for Lent once," the woman was saying, "and I was doing so good until I drank some hot chocolate!"

Aubrey looked past me, welcoming them. I stepped aside.

"You know you just don't think about there being choco-late in a drink," the woman continued. The man held up two fingers and laughed. Aubrey gestured for them the follow, and they did, the woman continuing to talk.

When she came back, I held up one finger. "What's that?" she asked.

"One," I said, "for the bar, if you have it."

"We can't afford to eat here," she said.

"I'll have appetizers. Or some an-tie-pasta," I said and grinned. As I said it, I became stuck on it. "You do have an-tie-pasta, right?"

She gave me a menu. "Seat yourself," she said.

As I was walking away, I heard her cheerfully greeting her next customers, a group of dark-suited men with valet tickets in their hands.

When I finished a "small plate" of ravioli, I went across the street to a dive bar and had four more beers. I sat near the jukebox and marveled at how effortlessly it switched discs.

* * *

We began sleeping and eating in relative solitude. The paper route had been our communal activity, and for months, it had sustained us. But now as the seasons changed, I began doing it alone. Aubrey had never been one for cold weather.

I began making sacrifices. They were unrequested, and largely, unnoticed. On mornings when it was particularly cold, I would be the one who roused from our cocoon. When she stirred, I told her, "You should stay here," but didn't mean it. I wanted her there, waiting for me when I leapt back in the car, the clouds of exhaust rolling past our windows.

I nearly lost it one night just before the route. I was eating some leftover gnocchi from her restaurant. In my pajamas. I was grateful she'd brought it home but knew from her posture and the frosted storm windows I'd be working alone later.

"They're calling for snow," I said.

"It was all anyone talked about at the restaurant," she said.

I searched for something else to say but failed. By the time I finished, she was already in bed.

Later, when the alarm went off, she pawed at it, unable to find the snooze button. Before she said anything, I was up; the crescendo of the alarm filled the house. She found the button.

"Would you mind?" she said, and I knew what she meant.

I said, "Sure," but dressed slowly, hoping she'd change her mind.

*   *   *

I was working alone two nights later when my car broke down. A hose ruptured somewhere in the cooling system. I could smell the antifreeze. I still hadn't forgiven Aubrey, so after pulling into a parking lot, I called my father. He sounded awake, as though he'd been waiting for such a call.

I told him my location. When he arrived, he glanced under the hood. "Looks like your water broke."

We were alone in the parking lot. Somewhere near its entrance, a flagpole rattled.

"Exactly what I was thinking," I said.

He grinned. And while I called a tow truck, he transferred the newspapers to his Crown Victoria.

"Do you want me to drop the car off in the morning? I can take the bus to work," I said.

"No, I might as well help you. How far behind are you?"

I hadn't thought of this, and it maddened me. My father was inanely practical.

The rest of the night, he drove and I delivered. On Memphis Avenue, he left me briefly and returned with two cups of coffee and a bag of doughnuts. "They gave me the doughnuts for free," he said. "I think they thought I was a cop."

I grunted and resumed stuffing the papers into bags.

"I was at your brother's house the other day. They're redoing the floor, so they've piled all the furniture in the bedroom. It looks like a moving truck backed through the wall and dumped its load," he said. "The floors are coming along though; he's rented quite a floor sander."

"Where he'd get it?" I asked.

"I don't know. Some equipment place. Sounded like he got a good deal."

"He doesn't know how to run one. He should pay someone to do it." "Apparently, it's user-friendly. He's been working at it on his days off."

I pictured my brother, dressed in a shirt and tie, trying to control a renegade sander. I laughed.

"How's Aubrey?" he asked.

"Good," I said. And when I didn't expound, he let it drop. We finished around six—late by all standards. My dad dropped me off and tried to give me money, but I refused. I went in through the French doors and started to crawl into bed but thought better of it. Instead, I waited until it was light, called the repair shop and left early for work.

I went the day without sleeping, and by the next night, I was scared that if I tried to sleep, I'd miss the route. I sat drinking coffee at the kitchen table until I heard the familiar thump of the papers.

I did the route from memory. And it wasn't until I was near its end that I realized I'd skipped an entire street. As I pulled into a driveway to turn around, a large green ball bounced behind my car. I hardly caught it in the backing lights, but as soon as I did, I floored the brakes. No one was around. I inched out slowly and looked down the street; the ball was still rolling. It was the type you might find in a bin at the supermarket. I looked the other way, suddenly concerned I'd see a kid chasing after it. But none came. And the ball finally came to rest on a sewer grate.

When I got home and finally slept, I became unsure it had happened. I tried to tell Aubrey about the ball, about how playful and incongruous it seemed on that dark street, but she barely listened.

"I'm sorry I wasn't there," she said.

* * *

A few days later, Aubrey came home early. I was busy sanding the floors in the narthex and didn't hear her. She stood outside the French doors and waited until I saw her before opening them.

"You're home," I said and tap-danced on a section of bared floor. "I wanted to surprise you."

"Where's our stuff?"

"It's in the bedroom," I said, "but don't worry; the landlord approved this."

She seemed to consider this. "I'll come back."

And when she did, I was finished. I'd swept the front rooms and put down the first coat of lacquer. I met her on the porch. "We'd better climb through the bedroom window," I said.

* * *

A week later, Aubrey finally rejoined me on the route. It was a balmy night, and she surprised me by already being up when the alarm went off. I found her in the sanctuary. She said, "The floors look good." She was already dressed. She said she'd drive.

We worked slowly, and largely, in silence. Halfway through, she said, "I think we should give it up."

I'd noticed her lack of urgency but had figured she was simply out of practice. "What do you mean?"

"I mean, what is this? We're stumbling through the route; we're both half asleep."

"The money's not bad though," I said. And it wasn't.

She was silent for a moment. "If you want to keep doing it, that's fine, but this is my last night."

As she said, it seemed as if a weight was lifted from her. She looked at me and smiled. "I'm sorry," she said. "It's silly to be dramatic about it. We just want different things."

My body contracted at the thought of doing it alone. I couldn't imagine it.

From that point, the route went well. She began to sing along with the radio, and whenever I got back in the car after making a particularly good throw, she'd pat me on the knee. "You're good at this," she said. And I wanted to believe her.

But at the start of the valley bridge, near the end of the route, my car died again. This time, I didn't call my father. We were out of gas. Aubrey seemed unconcerned. I attempted to mimic her nonchalance. "We'll leave it here for now," I said and began walking. "There's a place up the street. They'll be able to help."

It was a 24-hour service station where I often stopped in for coffee. She matched my pace but stayed behind a few steps. The air was foggy from melting snow, and when I looked over my shoulder, I could see only her form.

When we got to the station, I bought a gas can and filled it up at the pump. She stood inside and chatted with the cashier. "He's a college student," she told me when she came out, as though there could be nothing more romantic.

She offered to carry the gas can, but I wouldn't let her. When we got back to where the car should have been, it wasn't there.

"Well, I'll be damned," she said and laughed.

"What?"

"I mean, come on, it's kind of funny."

The gas can was still in my hand. I wanted to prove myself capable of a dramatic gesture, so I spun on my heel and threw it toward the top of the bridge's fence. It was a good heave, but even so, it caught the top of the wire and crashed back to the pavement. The cap shot off, and as the gas started glug-glugging out near the outer white line, Aubrey laughed.

I turned back to her. "You're lazy," I said.

In the darkness, it was difficult to translate her reaction, but it wasn't a surprise exactly. For a moment, she continued to smile, and it seemed to turn from merriment to marvel. I thought maybe she pitied me.

Desperate for some sort of response, I said it again. "You're lazy. You don't know what it means to work."

"We're not married, you know. We've just been playing house."

She stormed past me back toward the end of the bridge and turned left into the Metroparks.

* * *

We began walking again, but this time, I followed. She kept a strong pace, despite the wetness of the ground. I said, "We should call a cab," but she didn't respond. I said, "We shouldn't cut through here," but it went unanswered. During the day, we'd occasionally gone for walks in the park, but it was dark now and this was not the same park.

We pressed on, forging a road where there was none. It hardly seemed fair. When I felt myself grow winded, I called her name, but the air was dense. It had become a place without echoes. I could see her shadow cutting between the trees, could hear her footsteps sloshing in the snow.

"Why do we have to keep your pace?" I said, but I knew there wasn't hope.

My feet were numb. I thought of a nearby church camp I'd once attended with my brother. The director had insisted the woods were "God's backyard" during a night hike, and yet, here was a moment that resembled it and there was no god to be seen.

But if there was a miracle that night, it was that she was headed home. Before I realized where we were, we were climbing out the other side of the valley. I recognized the landmarks but couldn't see Aubrey. I walked our street slowly. When I came close enough, I saw the porch light was on. I took it as a good sign, but I didn't want to go in. I looked at our house, and it struck me as remarkable that anyone had ever attempted to have a church there. There was no steeple. No grandeur. There was little to separate it from the other houses in the neighborhood.

After a minute, she came out onto the porch and stood so her figure occluded the porch light. With the fog, she didn't notice me. She didn't call my name as I hoped she might, and when I didn't call out to her either, she seemed to sigh before retreating inside.

I waited and then climbed the steps. Her shoes lay by the door, just on the edge of our ironic doormat. Wet and muddy, they pointed outward, as if ready for exodus.

My brother had laughed when he helped us move in. "This could never be a church," he'd said. And now, through the window, I saw how claustrophobic it must have been—not nearly enough room for a group of believers and their god. At least not a big god.

In that moment, though, it didn't seem shameful that they'd tried.

THE MACHINE WE TRUST

On the fifth day of unemployment, the idea was born. My roommate, Fritz, and I were watching TV, still not speaking when a special came on about the history of polygraph machines. I wasn't sure Fritz was awake until he said, "How about that?"

It was the first he'd really spoken since Wednesday. Given the heat and our lack of AC, he hadn't put on pants since Friday.

"What's that?" I asked.

He didn't answer. I turned back to the TV. I cradled a lukewarm freezer burrito in my lap. On the screen, there was a shot of a polygraph machine: it sat on a desk in a darkened room and was lit by a spotlight. A b-list celebrity voiced over: "And yet the polygraph remained the authorities' primary weapon against suspected communist sympathizers."

The camera moved toward the machine and rose above it to give the viewer an overhead view. It was clear that the machine was supposed to be as glamorous as it was sinister.

The celebrity said, "Despite challenges to its reliability, the polygraph remains the machine we trust to uncover the truth."

It was the last line of the special, and when it ended, I moved to the kitchen. Fritz was already there, feeding his leftover cola to the aloe plant. His other hand was hooked into the side of his tighty-whities. Combined with his undershirt and mustache, he seemed to be channeling a Cold War housedad.

"How hard do you think it is?" I asked.

"What?"

"The polygraph machine. I mean, if the Russians could teach themselves to do it—"

"The Russians are a hardier people," he said. "But it's really about overcoming yourself, Caldwell." He never used my first name, and I tried not to resent it. "You shall know deceit, and deceit shall set you free," he said. He cracked another cola and allowed the first sip to dribble into the plant. "The last and the first to the earth."

"So, you think it could be done?"

"One can do almost anything with the right machine, some resolve, and a few well-timed Adderall. Do you have any dried basil around here?"

I nodded. "Above the stove. Go easy on it." We hadn't even been unemployed for a full week and already supplies were beginning to run low. "I'm going to beat it," I said, thinking of the polygraph test.

Fritz grunted in a way I interpreted as approval. He said, "It's better than trying to run a marathon. That's what most white people do when they're short on accomplishments."

* * *

I promised myself it wouldn't be like other pet projects I'd tinkered with and abandoned over the years, like when I'd tried to teach myself to pick locks and write left-handed. My curiosity often surpassed my follow-through.

Passing a polygraph test was tangible, and even though I wasn't sure how I would put my skills to use, lying seemed like the key to inaccessible worlds—to politics, to sexual promiscuity, to jobs that paid a living wage. I'd read once that a hallmark of working-class people—or let's be honest, my people—is their discomfort around authority. The ability to lie, I couldn't help but think, might be key to transcending that.

As for promiscuity, the truth was that I'd been with only one person and that was only because she found out she'd be the first—a compassionate pioneer as it were. Her name was Michaela, and she'd been my date to the campus formal my last year of college. She wore a gauzy yellow dress and spent a good portion of the night dancing, without me, near a spotlight that made her silhouette the filament within a translucent dress.

When I finally joined her for a couple songs, I said, "Did you plan this?" meaning the combination of dress and light. I thought it was bold and sensational, especially since I was forever showing up in places with blacklights only to discover stains on my shirts. I couldn't imagine nailing a moment like she was.

"What are you talking about?" she asked.

I blushed. I didn't want her to feel embarrassed or self-conscious if she didn't know, and even though I hadn't meant to notice, I felt a bit foolish and was worried she'd think I was skeezy. What I really wanted to say was: *That made me want to be you.*

"The spotlight was really accentuating your, uh, moves." I pointed over toward the light. Instead of being embarrassed, she acted upset, but I got the feeling that wasn't quite it.

She said, "Wait, were you watching me?"

I played it honestly. I didn't know any other way. "I mean, I was. Is that okay?"

"What did you see?"

I didn't want to say, but I stammered into a partial explanation. When I'd suffered long enough, she smiled. "You're a virgin, aren't you?" When I didn't say anything, she looked at me with pity and then pulled me close, even though we hadn't been dancing. "Well, that explains 'The Melancholy.' You just need to get laid."

It was supposed to be a joke, but I didn't laugh. Her comment, though, ensured sex was inevitable. It hadn't really occurred to me that the night might go that way, but it felt like abstaining would be impolite.

It was the first of a few times, all of which were fun, but by the time I lost my job, we'd stopped getting together. No breakup to speak of. We just got slower at responding to one another's notifications and when I suggested plans a couple of times, she told me she was slammed with work.

With the birth of the polygraph project, I fantasized that I might, if I someday wanted to, have many lovers. I couldn't picture who they would be, only that I would be a badass. Like Fritz.

* * *

When I lost my job, The Melancholy briefly set in. I'd been working at Shearer's Home Appliances, repairing and delivering large, neutral-colored Maytags and Hotpoints. Sometimes, I made repair calls. My coworkers liked to kid me about it, even though they did the same job.

"So, Artie, get laid today?" they'd say. Why they'd singled me out I couldn't understand.

I suppose the real trouble was that I accepted it.

"Yeah, any desperate Debbies?" This was Fritz's term. He worked there too. He thought himself ironic, yet part of what propelled him there was the faith that sometimes fetching, lovesick women ordered washer-dryer stacks to offset loneliness. His avowed goal was to "make it" with one on top of a delivered item. He publicized it well enough that everyone knew, including our boss. "I mean," he said, "I've fooled around on these calls, but never *on* the item."

When it finally happened, I took the fall with him. I'd been on the delivery and imagined we were operating under a sort of code—the one that leaves frat boys sleeping in cold lounges so their roommates can make it with dive-bar randoms or, in this case, waiting for ninety minutes in an idling delivery truck even though we wound up being overdue at the warehouse by a whole hour.

I was sure that Fritz would do the same for me.

"You're both fired," our boss said when we gathered in his office.

"But, sir," I said. "That truck's starter is garbage."

"Save me the shit, Caldwell. You've got a hammer. And, failing that, a phone."

The boss knew. Fritz's braggadocio after the event was unprecedented, even in our all- male workplace. Every-one else had basically slapped Fritz on the back or tried to one-up him with their own tales, but the real power, I felt, came from the fact that none of us could disprove him, even if we thought he was full of it.

"I don't know what you two were doing out there, but you're not my problem anymore."

Fritz, who had said almost nothing, finally spoke. "Oh, come on. I'm no cocksucker."

* * *

We were silent on our way out of the building, even as the staff made a de facto receiving line for Fritz. As we walked through them, Fritz took off his Shearer's work shirt and threw it over everyone's head and into the warehouse. Then, as if struck by a good idea, he did the same with his undershirt.

There were whistles and laughter. "Take it all off," some-one yelled, and so Fritz did.

By the time we stepped through the overhead door onto the loading dock, Fritz was in a pair of cheeky white Hanes. He stopped and pretended to wiggle out of them, mooning his audience briefly before pulling them back up.

"None of you ladies are pretty enough for the full show."

Someone threw a wad of packing tape at Fritz. He threw it back, and we walked down the stairs to my car.

Once we were clear of them, I said, "Rent's due next Tuesday." Fritz grunted.

I knew I maybe had enough in my checking account to cover it if I also sold my gaming console, so I didn't push it. He'd only been my roommate for half a year and co-workers for less than that. He was the ex-roommate of a friend who had found him through Craigslist. My friend had dogs and, in what was becoming a bit of a trend, had bought a house for himself and those dogs. Fritz moved in just as I was wondering how to keep my place. I'd rented it after graduation, under the impression that I was on some sort of upward trajectory.

As we drove back to the apartment, I didn't know what else to say, so I said, "That Mrs. Insley, right?"

Fritz leaned back in his seat and put a bent leg up on the side of the door like I'd noticed girls do while driving around town. "You know," he said. "We wouldn't have been late if she'd been satisfied doing it just once."

It was almost as though he was daring me to call his bluff, but I didn't. Fritz reclined his seat and closed his eyes. His lean body stretched from the backseat to the front windshield. It had a light sheen of sweat but didn't have the heinous tan lines that mine did, although I couldn't understand how. For just a second, I wondered what would happen if I reached over and touched him. I'd seen guys around the warehouse give each other ball taps and other homoerotic nonsense. If I was good enough, I imagined, I could lie and say I was joking.

Instead, I focused on driving. Red light, red light, yellow light, home. Once there, we sheltered in place, silently indulging in a food bender during which we cooked most of what I had in the refrigerator. It was the beginning of a pattern: for days, we scavenged and cooked but didn't talk.

*   *   *

Surprisingly, I found unemployment tolerable. I even began to enjoy the self-imposed austerity measures: the clipping of coupons, the diet of beans and rice, the abstinence from air conditioning and driving. The economy was supposed to be doing okay, but I couldn't figure out where the decent jobs were for folks who didn't possess two to five years of experience.

Yet we still watched cable TV. In Fritz's mind, it was hardly a luxury; rather, it was a necessary part of the American experience. He claimed that the government should provide it. "Like food stamps," he said. "For cultural nourishment."

Neither of us had much going, so when the polygraph project came about, it seemed a suitable alternative to having a regular job.

Of course, I had a hard time locating a machine, so after a few days, I began constructing my own. Online, I found distributors, many of which wanted personal information I was reluctant to disclose. It felt necessary to keep the project covert.

Constructing one wasn't totally out of my league. I'd once been an eagle scout—even though I never completed my final project—and I'd been repairing appliances for over a year. With the help of eBay, a medical supply site, and an anti-government kook in Illinois, I gathered enough materials to begin. I set up a workstation on top of the washer and dryer and hung a bare bulb above the operation like a spotlight. As I worked, the parts clinked and clacked against the metal in a way that helped me feel like I was getting somewhere even when I wasn't.

I got less and less done every day. And then, one week, I hit a complete impasse. I also didn't know how I was going to make rent. I'd been working some as a Handy through a website called Here & Handy, but our city wasn't that big, and most of its residents were too old and Midwestern to outsource menial tasks through their phones.

One afternoon, Fritz came home with a new job. I wouldn't have known except that he was dressed in medical scrubs.

"What's up with the outfit?" I said.

"The laboratory mandates it," he said.

"How'd you get that gig? You don't have any medical experience."

"It's animal testing."

"Still," I said. "You must have lied pretty fierce."

"Caldwell, one doesn't have to lie unless the right questions are asked. And besides, all they care is that I pass the eye test and say I can do the job."

He moved to the kitchen. I'd been watching a special on the history of the Third Reich, but I flipped over to cable news. Soon, The Frustration was upon me. Either it was impossible to tell deceit from truth, or the world wasn't interested in trying.

When Fritz came back, he had a cola in one hand and some metal parts in the other. "Why were these in my whites load?"

I vaguely remembered discarding some odds and ends into the washer basket the day before, mostly for the acoustic payoff, but I didn't feel like apologizing.

"Maybe they were in your pocket," I said.

"Maybe they weren't."

"It shouldn't be a problem much longer," I said. "I'm almost done. I've never built a polygraph before, but I'm pretty much dominating it."

"Really?" he said. "You're still on that?"

* * *

Later that week, I called Michaela. I couldn't have told you why. I guess I just wanted to update someone on my progress. Fritz seemed dubious, if not indifferent.

She answered on the third ring, and in the background, I could hear water sloshing around. "What are you up to?" I asked.

"I'm just leaving kickboxing. What do you need?" She didn't believe in reciprocated questions. It was one of her policies.

"Nothing," I lied.

"Then why are you calling, Arthur?" She was one of the only people to call me by my first name, and while I was grateful for this small bit of dignity, she refused to use "Artie" which is what I'd always preferred.

"I'm teaching myself to lie. I thought maybe you could help."

"What would make you think that?"

"I wasn't accusing," I said. "It's just something I'm doing. I'm building a polygraph machine."

"Why?"

I didn't want to explain. "It seems like the only way to do it right."

She paused. The sloshing on the other end grew louder, then ceased. "Well, I know where one is," she said. "That is, if you get tired of playing around."

* * *

We took her car. Fritz rode in the back, and since he was just home from work, wore his scrubs. Michaela drove the whole way one-handed, smoking a cigarette with her free hand. "You know it's all quackery, right?"

"That's what I told him," Fritz said, although he hadn't. "A lie that traps lies. Rich stuff."

"Still, it's a formidable obstacle," I said. "Where are we going?"

"You'll see," she said.

We rode silently for a while, listening to some kind of femme rock that included a sitar. I was experiencing The Rage until Fritz finally leaned between the bucket seats and yanked out the aux cord. "That's enough bullshit," he said. I thought Michaela might contradict him, but she didn't. Perhaps it had all been ironic to begin with.

We arrived a few minutes later in front of an old civic building, a blockish multi-use mass of concrete that had housed, in its various incarnations, a postal sorting center, a juvenile detention center, and a theatre space.

Michaela led the way through the alley to the back of the building. Fritz followed. I trailed behind. "It's in a back closet," I heard her tell Fritz. "I saw it when I worked crew for *Whispers of Me*." After college, she'd volunteered for a youth theatre group.

"Fritz was just telling me the other day about how he hates theatre," I said, more passive- aggressively than intended.

"Oh yeah?" Michaela asked, looking over at Fritz.

He shrugged.

On the backside of the building, we found a door pinned shut by a dumpster, which we pushed out of the way despite tremendous protest from its wheels. Fritz pulled on the door handle until it finally gave and he crashed backward into Michaela, nearly knocking them both over.

"You okay?" Fritz asked.

Michaela had caught herself, I noticed, by grabbing hold of Fritz's back. Her hands lingered as she assured him that she was.

"After you," Fritz said to me. "Enlightenment awaits."

* * *

The section of the building we were in hadn't been fully used in years. There was a heavy layer of dust over everything. A large pirate ship dominated the room, and along one wall was a jungle backdrop, complete with monkeys and an oversized jaguar slinking through brush.

"What kind of theatre did they do here?" Fritz asked.

"Adolescent. It was therapeutic," Michaela said. "We were trying to help keeps kids find healthy expression."

"Sometimes the healthiest way to be yourself is to be someone else," Fritz said. Michaela laughed.

"You can't really believe that," I said.

Fritz shrugged. "How's being yourself working out for you?"

We pushed further into the room. There was a euphemism for what we were doing that was escaping me. It wasn't trespassing. It was urban exploration. I wondered what we'd say if someone caught us.

At the far end of the prop room, we found the closet. Its door was off its hinges. Fritz stepped forward and moved it out of the way. "Eureka," he said after a minute. "Seek and ye shall find." Inside the closet were a couple sets of metal shelves—full of paint cans and various pieces of hardware. Most of it was junk, but unmistakably, on the second shelf sat a polygraph machine.

"Is it real?" I said, but somehow, we all knew it was.

"Let's get you hooked up, brother," Fritz said.

"I don't know if I'm ready."

"Only half of achievement is being prepared," he said. "Have a seat. I'll bring out the machine."

Fritz carried the machine out by the jungle backdrop, with little regard for the fragility of it. Yet, given his work scrubs and trademark surety, he seemed well-cast.

I sat next to the jaguar as he began hooking me up. "You're already sweating, Caldwell," he said as he attached the sensors. "You're never going to pull this off."

"You're probably right," I said.

"Don't let yourself talk like that," he said, looking at me fully for what seemed like one of the first times ever. Was this meaningful? It was hard to tell in the poor lighting. "I was just messing with you," he said.

Michaela watched from near one of the narrow windows. She was a silhouette against the late evening light. She was smoking a cigarette. "You ready?"

Fritz moved away from me, taking up station on an old love seat a few feet from me. He flipped a switch and the machine whirred to life, humming softly with electricity.

I let out my breath.

She stubbed out her cigarette against a piece of lumber. "We'll begin with some control questions, Fritz." Then to me, a rush of questions: "Is your name Arthur?" "Do you live in a house?" "Do you eat red meat?" "Have you ever stolen anything?" "Do you find me attractive?"

I answered honestly and as easily as I could manage. Every other question, I bit the side of my mouth; I knew this was the part where I should be using such tactics. To the last question, I admitted "yes" only after glancing at Fritz. He was busy studying the readouts. He had found a pen somewhere and was marking on the paper. He was taking his task seriously. When I finished answering, he studied the chart for a minute and then gave Michaela the thumbs up.

"Good," she said. "Now, for the fun."

She began pacing.

"Have you slept with anyone besides me?"

I looked again at Fritz. He was staring at the machine in puzzlement. Or perhaps expectation.

"What? Have you?" I asked.

"You can't repeat questions."

"Yes."

I looked at Fritz. I hadn't thought to do anything during my response, although in this moment, I wasn't sure what I should've done. After a pause and a couple marks with his pen, he looked up. "He's lying," he said.

It was the first real question, and I had missed it. "Try it again," I said. I could feel that my face was flushing. I thought maybe I could try it again. With backwards arithmetic.

"No," she said. "We're finished. You're not ready for this."

"And what about you?"

"What about me?"

"Let's see you do this."

She lit another cigarette. She seemed to be appeasing me. "Fine."

Fritz hooked her up to the machine. I watched with jealousy at the easy physicality between them. He gently touched her, hooking on the sensors and blood pressure gauges. When he finished, I took the role of interrogator. I had a hard time thinking of questions. "Is your favorite food chicken cordon bleu?" "Did you once work at a sports bar called Mallard's?" and "Have you ever lied before?" before gaining momentum and leaving the control questions.

"Do you find me attractive?"

"You can't ask that. It's a repeat."

"Do you find me attractive?" I asked again. I was violating the rules.

"No."

I looked to Fritz. He flashed me a thumbs up, apparently without realizing what he was doing.

"Do you find Fritz attractive?"

"No."

I waited for his response, but none came. "Was that a lie?" I asked. I suppose it was to either of them. Fritz ignored me, and instead, glanced briefly up at Michaela. I allowed a long silence to settle myself. Neither of them spoke until I did.

"Are you a communist?" I asked. I couldn't have explained why.

"Yes."

Fritz looked down and studied the sheet. "It's true," he said.

It was clear that I was in the middle of a game—one with implied rules, one that I was never going to be very good at. But, as upset as I was, I couldn't help being impressed by how adept she was at manipulating the truth. It was almost grotesque. I walked over to Fritz and looked down at the paper, watching the needles bounce fluidly over it like racing speedboats.

"You're no Russian," he said to me.

Up until that moment, I had been thinking he would take a turn too. There was so much that I wanted to ask him: about his past, his afternoon with Mrs. Insley, his sexuality, but I realized then that it was a bit hopeless. I could ask, yet even if I got the questions right and used the machine, I knew I might never draw any closer to the answers.

"Are you taking a turn?" I said, because it seemed I should ask.

Fritz turned to face me. "I'm an open book," he said.

Michaela laughed.

Somewhere in the other room, we heard a door open and close. It was time to leave. Michaela removed the controls. Fritz boxed things up for me, and I carried it all back as we wound through the maze of props. They moved far enough ahead of me that I couldn't hear their whispered conversation. I struggled to catch up, but the pathway was dark, and the polygraph grew heavy in my hands.

TRIVIAL

My grandfather's dying wish was for me to appear on the nationally renowned quiz show, *Trivial?* For the past couple weeks, they'd been advertising tryouts for the upcoming teen tournament. "Ben," he said, "I need you to do this for me—and your father."

He was lying on what we'd assumed was his deathbed, a cot in the family room which had easy access to both the TV and the front porch. He was a smoker, a fact our family discussed as seldom as we discussed the developing world, and he thought he was dying. He told us as much but refused to go in for tests. "It's like facing a firing squad," he told me. "You don't need to know which bullet kills you."

I don't know what he told my parents, but I believed him.

When his cough diminished, and his appetite returned, I suppose some of us were more surprised than others. Dr. Dwight, who went to church with us, finally made a house call and declared my grandfather as healthy as the president.

"False alarm," Grandpa said.

When Dr. Dwight left with a coffee cake, Grandpa grew serious and called me over to his bedside and into his cloud of VapoRub. "This doesn't mean you're off the hook," he said.

* * *

Even before he got really sick, whenever we watched *Triv-ial?*—an almost daily ritual in our house—my grandfather would summon up a base level of theatrics that I found nearly as interesting as the show itself. He'd prop himself up on his cot in order to shout out irrational answers and berate the game's mustached host whenever he lapsed into a phony accent or tried to push through a weak joke. It wasn't my grandfather's show. He was only there because he was a guest in his son-in-law's house, and his son-in-law watched religiously, even when the show labored through special-interest tournaments for everyone from teachers to military veterans. Given his reduced mobility and diminished eyesight, Grandpa rarely left the house and therefore watched television incessantly, but it was the only show for which he roused himself—in large part, I realize now, because he could be sure of an audience.

Everything was a joke with my grandfather. On the rare occasions he still drove, it was usually because I needed to be ferried to and from a dentist appointment or retrieved after a rare invitation to a friend's house. I seldom went anywhere interesting. As he drove us home, he would act lost, missing turns and ignoring my navigational pleas. I was too old for that sort of thing, but indulging him didn't really cost me much, and I was always relieved when he broke character and steered us home. It proved to me he was still of sound mind, far enough from dementia that he was able to satirize it, even if his body was betraying him.

No matter how far we'd driven, we'd inevitably arrive home in time to find my father sitting straight-faced in front of the TV with his post-dinner can of Tab, waiting for the show. "You almost missed it," he'd say, and he'd rise from his chair to get his popcorn, as though he'd been saving bleacher seats at a ball game and was only now free to move about or use the restroom.

Perhaps it was the routine that my father liked, the consistency of the same show coming on every night, the same host dressed in the same palette of masculine blues and telegenic neutrals, but I think it was something more. My father was an electrician, a man of good intention and criminally modest ambition. He'd been an apprentice, never a student of formal education. The show was forever trying to trumpet the democratic nature of the competition through awkward, mid-round banter, in which the host descended on each of the contestants in turn, forcing them to share travel mishaps, celebrity encounters, or offbeat hobbies as though everyone watching was dying to hear about it. My father never missed this part, and he took special interest, I could tell, in what their occupations were. There was real allure for him in testing his mettle against professors, stockbrokers, or engineers. Once, when a former astronaut went on the show and didn't qualify for the final round because his score was too low, my father casually brought it up weeks later, as though he'd been thinking about it ever since.

"You should do it," my father said when I told him about Grandpa's request. "I think you might learn a lot."

These were, of course, my own words coming back to haunt me. I knew this was the rhetorical appeal to which my father was most vulnerable. I would often ask to go places—to concerts, to movies, to the beach—under the guise of education. "They're poets," I'd say and proceed to tell him how a band's lyrics had been inspired by obscure Native American poetry. To his credit, I don't think he ever quite believed me, but my mother was usually on my side. She wanted me to get out and experience the world. She was uncomfortable with me being around the house too much, and after he moved in, with me being around Grandpa too often.

My father signed me up, and even though my mother disapproved of the show—she often ran the blender during the nightly airing of *Trivial?*—she thought it would be a good experience. "When I was young," she said, "I wanted to be on *Star Search*, but I was never encouraged."

* * *

The week of the audition, we headed into Louisville. In the initial casting call, the show bragged that they "might be coming to a city near you," which meant they were driving around flyover country pulling something called the Trivia Trailer. It looked like the sort of thing you might find at a construction site. My grandfather: "When you get in there, they're going to try to intimidate you." My father: "When you get in there, they're going to try to trick you."

Neither was quite correct.

The room was full of a half dozen kids my age or so. They all seemed like they knew each other, and for a moment, I felt like I'd stumbled into a clubhouse. There didn't seem to be any adults present.

"This is my fifth time," a boy along the wall said. He wore a cardigan and glasses and drank from a Styrofoam cup. "I don't know what I did wrong last time, but I'm hoping the sixth time's a charm."

A boy listening to the cardigan boy wore similar clothes and also had a Styrofoam cup.

He chewed on his, teeth marks visible all around the cup's rim.

"What are you drinking?" I asked.

They looked up at me but said nothing. I moved to a coat rack in the corner and took off my jacket. It was a hand-me-down from my father. It wasn't something I normally thought about, but the rack was full of pea coats. I crossed the room and looked at a table they'd set up for food. There was a punch bowl full of sodas and ice, a tray with cookie crumbs, and a coffee maker.

"Sorry, I took the last of the coffee," a girl said. She looked normal.

I left the table alone and sat on one of the folding chairs near the door. The others continued talking. I recognized a few of them from school; social misfits of the sort that delighted in routine office supplies, pencil sharpeners, and staplers. They were the sort that, instead of asking questions when they raised their hands, attempted to add factoids at the end of a teacher's lecture. "And did you know," they'd say and launch into a boring anecdote that would make us all late to our next class.

Truth was, I didn't mind the factoids, but I was never going to say so.

There's something you should know about me: I was born in a public library. It was, of course, an accident, and it was a story my mother told repeatedly. That day, she was running errands around town and had just left the pharmacy when the first contractions hit her. "I didn't want to bother anyone," she said, "so I ducked into the library." It's the part of the story only a Midwesterner could tell. "Before I could find a payphone to call your father, you'd arrived."

There are, of course, gaps both in the logic and chronology of this. My birth made the local paper's front page, and my mother even appeared on the six o'clock news looking—I'm told—more like she'd run a 5K than given birth.

* * *

The suited duo—a man and a woman dressed in navy— who interviewed me asked me things that seemed to have nothing to do with the show.

"Don't you want to know the only country with a non-rectangular flag?" I finally asked. "Or what landmark battle was fought in 1066?"

The man said, "That's not really what we're interested in."

"Tell us something about you," the woman said, "something you don't think is true of anyone else."

I paused. "My grandfather once broke his neck while building me a treehouse."

"Were you helping him?"

"No."

The man wrote something down on his sheet. The woman put down her pen. "Anything else? Anything about you?"

I tried again. "When we went to Lincoln's birthplace, I got kicked out for lying down on his feather bed."

"Why did you do that?"

"I was eight and I think I'd been reading a lot about osmosis."

This seemed to work for them, and so I added, "And when my uncle got married, I took a chunk out of the wedding cake before they could cut it."

The last one was a lie, but whatever guilt I might have felt was relieved by their nods. These, I began to understand, were acceptable anecdotes.

Back in the parking lot, I waited for my father and grandfather to pick me up. They hadn't wanted to pay for parking when they dropped me off, so they'd begun orbiting. I was to wait for them as one would a bus.

I must have just missed them on their last loop because I was still waiting when the suited interviewers broke for lunch. To pass the time, I'd started walking around, jumping off things—something my friends and I called aggressive walking—and the interviewers saw me doing this.

"What are you doing?" the man asked. I didn't know what to tell them.

"You're a skater, aren't you?" the woman said.

I was grateful. "Yeah, I guess you could say that."

"A skater," she repeated. She looked at the man, and he nodded.

"Maybe we'll see you later," he said.

* * *

A week passed before the show called. They didn't ask for me. Instead, my father and mother spent twenty minutes saying things like, "We understand" and "Yes, that'll be fine" and other bland affirmative statements. I paced the room while they talked. It didn't occur to me that they wouldn't have called if I hadn't made it.

Grandpa said, "We're going to have to practice your one-liners."

"For what?"

"For the show," he said. "We need to make you more interesting."

My father came into the room. "They want to speak with you," he said.

I picked up the phone in the other room. A voice I didn't recognize congratulated me and told me when the taping was to take place. "So, you'll come up to Chicago in two weeks."

I'd never been to Chicago.

When I got off the phone, my father didn't say much. He fidgeted with the wall calendar in the kitchen. "I don't know if I can get off work," he said. He wouldn't look at me. "But I want to be there for this."

My father was not one to take days off work, but there was a hope in his voice that, even now, seems heartbreakingly earnest. "And you're going to have to study. A lot of these kids are going to come from private schools, from families who go to art museums and operas."

What he didn't say was, "I want you to be able to compete with them," but I recognized what he wanted. He wanted to stand by while I held my own and possibly won. He wanted someone to say, "Yours are a smart and worthy people."

"I can do this," I said but didn't know if I believed it. My mother came by and patted me on the back.

* * *

Since part of the show was about wagering, the following week, my grandfather took me to a riverboat casino just across the state line. He asked me to bring along my own money.

We set up at the blackjack table. "How old's the kid?" the dealer asked.

My grandfather didn't bat an eye. "He's here in case I have a seizure. Unless you want to carry me out," he said.

The dealer looked around. Except for a few middle-aged women playing slots, the casino was empty. He shrugged. "Minimum bet's two dollars."

My grandfather looked at me. "Pay the man," he said, and I slid forward a chip.

Later, after we had lost all our money, I asked my grandfather, "What do we do now?"

He took me to the bar. The bartender had a shaved head and a goatee. He looked at my grandfather. "What'll it be?"

My grandfather ordered something I'd never heard of. He said, "If you were going on the adult version, we'd give you a quiz on your alcohol."

"But I'm not."

"No, you're not."

We sat for a while, and I played with the square cocktail napkin that sat in front of me. I looked down the bar and estimated how many napkins it would take to cover its surface.

My grandfather called the bartender back over. As he came down the bar, he whispered to me, "Watch." Then to the bartender, he said, "Tell him a story."

The bartender looked over at me. "I'm not into babysitting."

I spoke up. "My grandfather said you'd be someone who had interesting stories."

My grandfather patted me on the shoulder. He said, "Or tell us something interesting about yourself."

The bartender paused. At the other end of the bar, a woman in heavy makeup called for his attention, and he left us to attend to her.

I sat, slightly embarrassed at my grandfather's shenanigans. I wasn't sure what he was up to, so I asked.

"Wait and see," he said. "Someone tending a bar won't be able to resist that bait."

As we waited, my grandfather offered me a sip of his drink. It tasted like sour orange juice. "Don't tell your father," he said.

When the bartender returned, he announced, "I once held a world record."

"You see," my grandfather said. The bartender waited, probably expecting my grandfather to ask for elaboration or make his point. Instead, my grandfather said, "Can I get another one of these?"

And when the bartender walked away, scowling, all my grandfather said to me was, "You can drive a car, can't you?"

* * *

At school in the days that followed, I tried to coax similar stories out of my teachers. Not surprisingly, they responded, some more enthusiastically than others. My English teacher, Mrs. McCovey, told me about getting lost on a trip to Rome. Mr. Graves, my PE teacher, revealed that he was allergic to peanut butter and almost died when he was a child.

No one knew I was going to appear on *Trivial?* I began taking better notes, and when the know-it-alls raised their hands at the end of class, I sat still while the other students gathered their books and rummaged in their backpacks.

I began spending study halls in the school library, combing through dusty almanacs and reference books. I studied topographical maps of the ocean floor and outdated geopolitical maps of the Balkans. I memorized capitals and rivers and the presidents and their years in office. I browsed study guides for standardized tests that I wouldn't take for years. I don't know what I thought I was learning. There wasn't much chance I'd retain the information, and there was even slimmer hope that any of it would appear on the show, but it helped reassure me: I felt more knowledgeable. I felt smarter. And when Mr. Summerford told me he was into philately, I knew to ask which stamps were his favorites.

* * *

My father's version of a field trip was something different. One afternoon, he picked me up from school. "We're going to have to hurry if we're going to make it," he said.

I didn't know what he was talking about, but there was something irresistible in his voice.

My father wasn't prone to drama.

We headed to the interstate and made good time. We passed semis and sports cars indiscriminately, and my father tuned the radio to a classic rock station. We came to the edge of the city as rush hour was just picking up, going the other way.

"Are we going to a game?" I asked.

"Something like it," he said.

I didn't ask any more questions. What we were doing seemed fragile and reckless, like crossing a frozen lake without checking the ice. And even though no one had taught me, I knew acknowledging a miracle would end it.

At the theatre, the quiz bowl teams arrived on buses. We walked from a free parking lot a great distance and carried the soda cups from the fast-food joint where we'd eaten. The team members wore ties and blazers, many of which were monogrammed. I didn't know where they'd come from, so I asked my father.

"From money," he said.

Inside, the teams squared off in round after round of indecipherable questions. The teams buzzed in so early it was impossible to derive any satisfaction from their answers. My father sat on the edge of his seat and tried valiantly to act as though it was interesting, but it wasn't the same as it was at home with *Trivial?* They might as well have been speaking another language.

*   *   *

A couple of days before our departure, I asked my mother to take me to the library. The more I studied for the show, the more I wanted to go back and see. It seemed important that this was a part of my legacy and an important part of what I was doing.

"You have a bicycle," she said. She hovered over the sink, intent on the dishes she was washing.

"I know," I said, "but I thought maybe you could, you know, show me where I was born." It was something we did once on my birthday but hadn't done since. My mother had walked me around the library like a tour guide, ending in the basement stacks near an oversized dictionary. "Right here," she'd said. "This is where you entered the world." She'd pointed at a spot on the ground just in front of us. There was a high window above us; sunlight streamed in but just missed where we were standing.

"In the sunshine?" I'd asked. "No, just to this side of it."

Now, in the kitchen, I asked again. "You won't show me?"

She stopped washing, and I could hear the remaining dishes bobbing against the walls of the sink. She kept the dishcloth in her hand as she turned around. "You're going to be disappointed."

I shrugged. "I just thought it might inspire me as I go on the show."

She dropped the dishcloth back in the sink and rinsed her hands. "I thought you knew.

With all the research you've been doing at the library, I figured you must have looked the article up."

Just then, I heard my father coming into the kitchen behind me. I didn't turn around, but I could hear him fetch his popcorn and start it in the microwave.

"You coming to watch?" he asked.

"Sure," I said.

When he left, my mother said, "You were born in the women's restroom. First floor. Third stall from the left."

* * *

That night, we watched the show but muted the volume. My father said, "You need to practice buzzing in."

Grandpa said to my father, "But you are going to unmute it during the meet-and-greet."

My father nodded, and the game began. We read the few clues to ourselves, and when I didn't hit the coffee table to buzz in and answer, my father said, "That's okay. They're tough tonight."

They weren't tough, but something about the silence of the room made it impossible to speak. I sat on the floor in front of the couch and watched the contestants' mouths move without sound. When they didn't know questions and had to be told the answers, they twisted their faces in comedic caricatures of ignorance and frustration.

I couldn't take it. "Can we watch something else?" I asked.

My father didn't say anything. Grandpa said, "How about *Hollywood Squares*?"

My mother rescued us. "Maybe he's just a little burnt out," she said. Even with the sound off, we hadn't heard her come into the room.

"I suppose that's a good point," my father said. "He should save it for the real deal."

Later, my mother came into my bedroom to say goodnight. It was a ritual we'd forgone years ago. She sat on the edge of my bed and thumbed over the reference books I'd taken to keeping on my nightstand. I wasn't expecting a quiz, but she asked, "Who lost the 1928 presidential election to Herbert Hoover?" She asked, "What is the main ingredient in chewing gum?" She asked, "What eastern European nation is the world's leading exporter of apple concentrate?"

I looked at her. I answered, "Smith?"

"Which one?"

I wanted to pick a name from that era. "Irvin?" I guessed.

"Al Smith, chicle, Poland," she said.

I felt panic rising from somewhere in my chest.

My mother squeezed my shoulder. "Relax," she said. "You're not supposed to know everything."

But for the next two nights, I stayed up reading from my books. I hardly slept. The nights seemed to stretch on indefinitely as I crammed thousands of facts into my brain. On the second night, when I could no longer keep my eyes open, I stole a dishpan from the kitchen, filled it with ice, and read with my feet submerged. It was something I remembered from a history book; someone had done it but

I could no longer remember whether it was Ben Franklin, Mohandas Gandhi, or the Apollo astronauts.

* * *

I don't remember much of the drive to Chicago. My family was excited, but I couldn't keep awake and dozed off somewhere amid the sea of corn and beans that we had to cross to reach the city. I slept most of the way. I woke up to my father arguing with a valet. Drowsy, I looked out my window and up toward the skyscrapers that towered over us. It felt as though we'd settled to rest in the bottom of a canyon.

The show had put us up at a four-star hotel near the lakefront, but it was a hotel that wouldn't let my father self-park. He put up a valiant fight. Grandpa left long before the loss was conceded. He headed toward the hotel lounge, and my mother chased after him.

"Is there anywhere around here where I can park myself?"

The valet, a stork of a man in a sports coat, told him about the city lot a few blocks away.

He asked me, "You mind?"

We walked back to the hotel in silence. I was still tired and didn't have much to say, but my father kept giving me meaningful looks, and when I sneezed, he asked, "Are you coming down with something?"

"No, I'm just tired," I said. "But maybe some food would help."

We ate that night at a Greek restaurant. I picked at my food even though it was delicious.

Grandpa asked, "Do you know what animal has got your tongue?"

I could smell the alcohol on his breath. I said, "I'm just tired."

My mother changed the subject, and for the rest of the meal, we talked about what she wanted to see around the city.

After we finished eating and the waiters cleared our table, my father stood as though he was going to make a speech. "I don't want you to be nervous, but I bought you something."

I could feel Grandpa and my mother tensing on their side of the table.

He brought a large package from beneath the table. It was wrapped in plastic shopping bags. I stood up to take it from him. Inside, there was a blue blazer and a red-and-navy striped tie of the sort that I might wear if I went to prep school.

"Well?" he asked. In the light of the restaurant, in his suit jacket, my father looked alien and fragile. I wanted to tell him why they wanted me on the show, but I didn't know how I would begin to say it. And even though I hated the suit jacket, I was obligated to say something. "It's blue," I said. "I was thinking it would be red."

My father looked stunned for a moment. "You mean you expected this?"

"No, it's just that red is the color for luck in China, and it's what Tiger Woods wears on the final day of every tournament he plays." I watched as my father's face fell. I looked to the other side of the table for help, but none came. "I mean, I like it," I said. "It was just something dumb I was imagining."

My father sat back down. The waiter came by to rescue him.

"We'll take the check now," Grandpa said.

* * *

When we arrived at the studio the next day, they separated me from my family. Having been through some scandals, the show was determined to make fair play a cornerstone of the experience, and so we were diverted into a large conference room. Here, my parents signed some forms and we parted ways. My mother gave me a long hug. Grandpa gave me what he claimed was his lucky charm: a vulture skull on a chain. "It's for vision," he said and winked at me. My father didn't say anything. He shook my hand. He looked as though he might cry.

After they were gone, an assistant herded me past the "contestants only" sign and into the main dressing room. I was surprised at what I saw. Other than my own, there was not a sports coat to be seen, nor were any of the pencil-sharpener-loving guys from the initial interview. Everyone was unique. Normal. Diverse.

The suited duo from the interview came over to greet me. "Welcome to the big stage," she said. The man shook my hand. The woman appraised my outfit. "Is this all you brought?"

I managed to nod. She looked at the man.

"Maybe we have something in wardrobe," she said.

She passed me off to the man who led me into the next dressing room. There were piles of outfits strewn around the room. The man said, "You're a skater, huh? These might all be a bit big, but isn't that the way you all like it?" He chuckled. "I'll be back for you in five."

After he left, I scoured the piles. I wanted to believe I could find something in the stacks of clothes that could somehow construe the right identity. I imagined walking out on stage, the applause rolling like thunder around me, and somewhere on the other side of the cameras, a family watching, saying to themselves, "He's of us. He's for us."

But there wasn't much to choose from. Eventually, I found a plain hooded sweatshirt. I took off my blazer and put it on over my white shirt. I also found a pair of baggy jeans and put them on over my khakis. I messed my hair up and looked at myself in the mirror. I looked sloppy, so I went back to where I'd left the blazer and put it on.

When the man came back a moment later, he said, "We have to go." He looked at my attire but didn't offer comment. He led me by the shoulder out through the first dressing room to where the other contestants waited in the wings.

"You nervous?" one of them asked.

I was. I didn't say so. I tried to see out past the curtains to where we'd enter.

"Now watch your step, folks," the stage manager was saying. "We wouldn't want any of you to start off on the wrong foot."

I heeded his warning, and as I climbed the stairs to the stage, I kept my eyes trained on my feet. Somewhere above us, the show's theme music started up, drowning the chattering of the crowd. I followed the boy in front of me and emerged from the curtain. I expected to see my family somewhere nearby clapping eagerly and shouting encouragement, but I could not find them through the impenetrable wall of spotlights. As I took my place at the contestant podiums, I imagined my family on the other side of the lights, Grandpa's hands clenched like he was at a betting track, my mother scouring the program for my name, and my father stoic but attentive. I was their lead horse. I was their shot at glory. But I was a long way from knowing anything at all.

HONEY

The morning my car was stolen, I was standing in my kitchen eating ice cream. I heard it start; it was unmistakable. Car startups are signatures immediately identifiable by their owners, even if they can't be replicated for an audience—as mechanics often request.

I don't even think I looked out the window before I called the police.

"I'd like to report a stolen car," I said, realizing that I'd been rehearsing this line for years. "It's a white Dodge Stratus with a red driver's door and a for sale sign in the window."

I gave them more of the car's information, then some of my personal information. An officer showed up a little while later, glanced at the glass, and then sat in his cruiser for twenty minutes. They gave me a case number and promised to call me if something came up.

I paced the now-vacant parking spot in front of my house. The broken glass remained on the pavement. I imagined they'd smashed the side window. A car came up behind me and honked. They had their right turn signal on, already wanting the spot.

"I'm sorry. You can't park here," I said. "It's a crime scene." I realized I looked rather unofficial, wearing my girlfriend's bathrobe over my pajamas and carrying a mug of coffee. The driver, apparently a student from the nearby university, shot me an incredulous look and accelerated on past. Parking was scarce in our neighborhood. Car theft was rampant. The correlation seemed suspicious.

The immediate problem this posed was that I was scheduled to pick up my nephew from school that afternoon and would now need to make alternate arrangements. He was eleven and wouldn't be impressed if his uncle rolled up on a ten-speed and asked him to sit on the handlebars.

* * *

Unfortunately, the one person who could remedy this situation, my girlfriend, wasn't home when it happened. She rarely was home anymore, leaving me to suspect her of having developed a clandestine hobby of some sort. I was jealous of that sort of thing, which jeopardized our relationship since she was someone who believed in clear lines of demarcation when it came to individual interests. She was afraid we'd absorb each other, and on some level, I think I badly wanted to. When I found out about her beekeeping classes, for example, I fumed for a week before confronting her mid-session while she was smoking a hive.

She knew why I was there. "You're going to get stung," she said.

I didn't care. I stood over the hive and tried to help her. She pointed the smoker at my face and squeezed. The smoke was heavy, the kind you get when you burn brush and dead grass. My eyes watered. "Tessa, you're not making this easy," I said. I was having a hard time reading her facial expressions through my tears and her protective mesh veil, but I knew she was upset.

That evening, I made my own honey nut cheerios. After she left, I had learned a lot about swarm behavior and how just a modest dosage of well-directed smoke can placate an entire hive. I had extracted the supers, and as a treat, was allowed to take home half a pint of fresh honey in a bear-shaped squeeze bottle.

Tessa came home while I was still eating. She stood in silence just inside the door until I called out to her. "Honey, did you know honey never goes bad? They say if it granulates on you, all you have to do is microwave it."

She understood I was trying to make amends. We made love for the next hour.

"Just don't do that again," she said when we'd finished. She made it apparent that the apiary classes hadn't been that important to her, but we both knew I was bound to do it again. It was our game of hide-and-seek that had started once we moved in together and consolidated personal space: she would go hide somewhere in the city taking bassoon lessons or repairing clocks, and I would follow as quickly as I could put together the clues. It seemed romantic, but in retrospect, I might have just been bored.

And lately, with work and my fledgling hobbies, I hadn't had time for such things.

* * *

As of the morning my car was stolen, I'd been in the beekeeping business for about two months. Despite the neighbors' complaints, there were apparently no ordinances against what I was doing. In a university town that had done its best to encourage gardens and chicken coops, beekeeping was considered "backyard agriculture," and so I was free to keep my fourteen hives along my back fence. I reasoned with my neighbors. "I planted flowers to encourage self-sufficiency," I told them. "The bees have no need to leave this yard. So long as their queen is happy, they're happy."

But the truth was, sometimes, their queens weren't happy. Recently, while the Christiansens were vacationing in Arizona, one of my queens abdicated to their cherry orchard. Armed with a saw and a five-gallon bucket, I carefully retrieved the swarm by sawing off a branch and shaking the basketball-sized swarm into my bucket. I painted the stub on the tree brown—so as not to attract attention—then marched back over to the hives. Upon their return, the Christiansens didn't notice.

I called them, asked if they knew about my car being stolen. They said they didn't and apologized loosely for my misfortune. In my mind I was making connections, playing detective. I needed someone with a motive, lest the whole experience would be a waste, like a novel with a random, unsatisfying ending. I needed the butler to do it, not some jackass seeking a joyride. This stemmed not simply from novels, but partially from my faith in the world—namely that crime, by and large, didn't happen arbitrarily. Most people I knew who had had things stolen were either absent-minded or abrasive. The first would leave valuable things unguarded—windows open, doors unlocked, laptops in public places—while the second would simply irritate enough people that someone would finally exact punishment on them for being a knucklehead.

I knew I wasn't absent-minded.

* * *

When I was young, my mother diagnosed me with what she deemed to be "a curious streak," which I imagine I still have if I ever did. It was her way of graciously dealing with me when I noticed details she didn't want me to, like when she used to touch her hair while talking to Mr. Morrison. It was something I'd never seen her do anywhere else. He worked in the greenhouse where we went once a week to satisfy my mother's green thumb. I asked her why she seemed to like him so much when Dad called him "Fast Eddie" behind his back.

That was when she praised me. "You have a real curious streak," she said. She also patted my head, which she'd never done before.

When I picked my nephew, Jacob, up from school, I told him this story. I could see the back of his neck nodding as I pedaled behind him but couldn't gage his reaction.

"Couldn't we just walk?" he asked. He was heavier than expected, and I was having trouble steering the bicycle. With junior high around the corner, I refrained from any comments about his pudginess.

"We can't lose time walking, Jake. I have a mystery to solve."

"Left! Left! Now!" he called from the front.

I strained at the handles and leaned. A car screeched its tires as it slowed down for us.

* * *

The police weren't very helpful in my investigation. After a week and a half, their promised call hadn't manifested. I was expecting them when I finally did get a lead. A man called me, having seen the "for sale" sign in the back window of my car. He was interested in buying.

"Where did you see it?" I asked.

"On Devonshire. Is it true what you said about low mileage? I was just wondering. Looks like an old model."

"No, that's right. It only has about 120 thousand," I found myself saying. "You should understand though—"

"And that door? What happened to the old one? An accident?"

"No, there was no accident. The door came off when I backed it into a curb." So maybe I was a little absent-minded.

"The new door came from the same model car; it just needs some new—"

"And the muffler?"

"What about it?"

"There isn't one."

"Sure, there is. It needs to be replaced, but the rest of the exhaust system is intact, and relatively new at that." I couldn't have explained why I felt so defensive. "Hey, are you interested in the car or not?"

"Well, I am if you're willing to replace the windshield first."

I was silent just long enough for him to hang up. Obviously, the windshield was a new development.

After he was gone, I realized what had happened. I tried using reverse call-back to talk to him again. I was sure he was either the culprit or someone in cahoots with him, and I was desperate to give him a piece of my mind. When the voice on the other end answered, "Howard's Stone Oven Pizza," I hung up.

* * *

By the time Tessa came home mysteriously out-of-breath and stood over the kitchen sink downing tap water by the glassful, I was angry, mostly with myself.

"Where have you been?"

She shrugged.

"My car was stolen this morning," I said.

"Oh?"

I told her about the phone call, and she seemed to listen as mere appeasement. When I finished, she said, "It was a piece of shit anyway."

I thought back to Christmas and the "don't laugh it's paid for" front license plate she'd given me as one of my first presents; it seemed hypocritical. And yet, as I tried to act offended, I knew she was right.

I said, "Look, if he calls back—"

"Tell him the price."

"No. Find out where he saw it."

"What good would that do?" she asked.

Again, a valid point; her rationality was vexing.

"Where were you anyway?" I asked. She was on her fifth glass of water and was munching on a handful of salted peanuts.

She didn't respond, and instead pushed past me with a smile on her way to the shower. Halfway down the hallway, she lifted her hands above her head and took off her shirt: an obvious taunt.

I retired to the living room and tried to reconstruct the crime. I envisioned the collage that was to take shape above my desk, complete with a large map, hemmed in by photos of evidence and suspects. With lots of yarn strung between them. I found a map and circled Howard's Stone Oven Pizza.

*   *   *

When I arrived there the next day, I was wearing an old deerstalker and a matching tweed suit—both of which I had found in our hall closet. I wanted to seem eccentric because I knew I wasn't going to seem official. While I was rummaging, I noticed our old metal checkerboard was missing—the one with feet and razor-sharp brass trim. I suspected Tessa, but having no time for another mystery, I abandoned it.

I entered, stopping for a moment to doff my hat to an exiting patron. Inside the walls were covered in memorabilia from Graceland. "You must be Howard," I said to a man behind the counter. He was pudgy and had been wiping his hands on his apron. He stopped as I stared.

Who wants to know? Was his line, but he neglected it.

"Where did stone oven pizza get started?" I asked. I had worked to refine my cloak-and-dagger approach on the bus ride over.

He shrugged; I'd asked innocently enough.

"Were you the one who called about the muffler-less Dodge Stratus?" It was a peace offering, and from his reaction, I thought he must be. "Were you still interested?"

"It wasn't me. It was one of our delivery guys, Paulie." He yelled this name into the back, and after a second, a younger, apronless man popped his head around one of the shelving racks.

"You fix the windshield?" he asked before I could say anything. "No, not yet."

"Well then, how much 'as is?' I normally wouldn't buy it that way, but it drove so nice, I think—"

"Drove?"

"Yeah, your brother let me take it for a test drive. I think the missing muffler actually gives it more road presence, as I'm sure you understand."

"That wasn't my brother," I said.

"You sure? Sure looked like you, didn't he, Sid?" he asked, nudging the man with the apron, who had been wiping his hands again.

"My hands get oily sometimes when I'm away from the flour for too long," he said. This felt like a threat.

"You tellin' me to leave? My brother wasn't here."

"How do you know?"

I stopped. I didn't know. For all I knew, it could have been my brother. It suddenly seemed plausible.

* * *

I called my brother from a pay phone in Little Italy; this too would have to be marked on my map when I got home. He answered on the third ring and denied everything.

"What do you mean? He said that?" he asked, sounding a bit too incredulous for my liking.

"Yeah, he did. What were you doing yesterday?"

"How's Tessa? You guys doin' okay?" A deliberate subject change.

"Yeah, we're fine. Hey, can we get together tomorrow for lunch?"

"Sure, of course."

After we hung up, I replayed the conversation. I found myself wondering why he'd changed the subject instead of offering an alibi.

* * *

At home, I went to check on my bees. Recently, mites had been infesting the hives, and I'd been losing swarms regularly. The number of brown stumps in the Christiansens' backyard increased. Their trees were beginning to look pollarded. Typically, I waited until dusk, then snuck out and cut the branches. Once or twice they heard the sawing and I had to leave mid-task. Once, in the beginning, Tessa caught me, revealing her position through a complex series of bird calls we'd once memorized together from a nature special on PBS. She was wearing binoculars and a velour jogging suit. And when the Christiansens' back door opened, we slipped through the shadows to the edge of our own yard and made lewd noises until it shut again.

That was the only time. The real problem was sometimes the bees weren't taking to the hives when I brought them back, and even when they did, honey production was dismal. I was failing as a beekeeper, it seemed. I redoubled my efforts, checking them more often, making unscheduled visits—as I did today—during which I imagined I might catch the bees in some sort of secret behavior that would allow me insight into their battle with the mites. With my brother still on my mind, I carefully lifted the tin cover off the hive and peered in; I hadn't brought my smoker.

A few of the more curious bees flew out. The state of affairs inside the hive looked normal, except that upon lifting out one of the supers, I could see there was little honey. I let it slide back in place. I could feel a couple bees hovering above my right ear, nestling in my hair. I tried to waft them away, but with no luck. One stung me on the top edge of my ear.

*　*　*

"Bees only sting once," Tessa said when I entered the back door rubbing the side of my head. "It's a shame he wasted himself on you."

It was an ambush. She was leaning against the refrigerator completing a crossword puzzle in red ink.

"You were watching that?" I asked, moving toward the baking cabinet. "The mites are wreaking havoc on them. I'm losing nearly a swarm a week." I extracted a spoonful of baking soda from its box and begin mixing it with water: an old home remedy I'd learned about in class.

As I leaned forward and applied it, I noticed Tessa was barefoot and wearing black tights that were visible below the bottom of her jeans.

"What's that about?" I asked, vaguely gesturing at her cuffs.

"Maybe I'm cold," she said. "What is a four-letter word for 'deep urges'?"

"Beats me. I hate crosswords."

157

"It's because you're terrible at them. It's *yens*."

"Did you look that up?"

She didn't respond, except to twirl her pen victoriously.

"Hey, I want to have lunch with my brother tomorrow. I think he might have been responsible for my car being stolen. You want to come?"

"I can't," she said as she backpedaled into the other room.

* * *

I met my brother at a diner on Western Ave. I'd prepared a short list of questions with which to ambush him. I settled into the booth and ordered a root beer. I taped the questions to the inside of one of the menus.

He arrived a few minutes later. He'd brought Jacob, which didn't help anything. They plopped down across from me, which caused the cushion to exhale flatulently and Jacob to laugh.

"So, what's this you wanted to ask me about?" my brother asked after we exchanged pleasantries. "You sounded upset over the phone. Is everything alright with you and Tess?"

I took a long sip on my soda to collect myself. "Yes, everything is great with Tessa, but my car's—"

"Hey, look at this," Jacob said, holding up a piece of paper. "I found this taped to the inside of my menu."

I felt my face turning red. I started to speak up when the waitress came back for our orders. "Whatcha got there?" she asked, looking at Jacob.

"I don't know. It was in my menu. Is it yours?" he asked, looking up at the waitress.

She took it from him, glanced at the questions, scoffed in the direction of the floor and pocketed it. Damn her. Damn Jacob's honesty.

I ordered an open-face roast beef sandwich. My brother and Jacob both got fish and chips. As we waited for the food, I tried to regroup. "So, my car—"

"Jacob, stop that!" my brother nearly yelled. Jacob had begun squeezing ketchup onto a short stack of napkins. It was flooding onto the table. "It's for my fries," he explained.

"My car's been—"

"You need mustard," he said, grabbing the yellow bottle from beside the napkin holder.

He squirted Jacob's arms with it.

"Hey," Jacob said, aiming the ketchup at his dad.

"Don't you dare—" my brother started before a spray of ketchup hit him across the top of the shirt.

Mild chaos ensued. My brother grabbed for a ketchup bottle on a nearby table, and Jacob, seeing this, crawled over the high back of our booth to get away from him. There was a couple eating at the next table over. Jacob either misjudged his landing or lost his footing and landed on one of their omelets.

*   *   *

When we were asked to leave, I asked my brother to drop me back off at Howard's Stone Oven Pizza. To his credit, I had to give directions.

The pudgy man immediately recognized me. He called to the back, "Hey, Paulie, it's for you," and then began ignoring me as if I were a ringing phone.

Paulie emerged from the back, took one glance at me and tried to put me back on hold. "Give me a second. I have to get my checkbook."

"Checkbook?" I asked, suddenly alarmed.

"Yeah, your brother came by yesterday. He sold it. Paulie talked him down though, like a good boy. You don't mind of course, do you?"

We locked eyes across the counter. I leaned forward. "Just how far?" I said.

He shrugged but maintained eye contact. "Your brother said you wouldn't mind on account of the bashed-in windshield. That must have been quite a deer you hit. Said the way you told it the bastard ran into you."

As Paulie came back wielding a thin blue book and a pen, I looked at him. He was in the process of signing it. "Twenty-one hundred, yeah? Do you mind a personal check?" My silence must have stopped him. "I swear it's good. Your brother said that he only wanted three hundred dollars and that I was to pay the rest to you. He left this envelope for you, too, said you'd be by for it."

I took it from him and opened it. Inside was an assemblage of receipts for two tanks of gas, a pair of department store jeans and a day and a half of fast food. Something grease had made illegible was scrawled on the back of an Arby's receipt, but I could tell immediately that it was Tessa's handwriting. The last was the clearest; it read *later*. Or *taker*. Or *tater*. I couldn't tell.

* * *

As was to be expected, I was in a celebratory mood as I unlocked the door to our apartment. I was eager to congratulate Tessa on her surprise, so when I found it silent, I was more disappointed than alarmed. For the first time in days, I became curious where she was. I looked around for clues and began noticing her things were missing—most ominously the vintage suitcase that she'd always kept on the top shelf of our closet.

I made a cup of coffee and went out into the backyard. I sat facing the hives with my back to the city. I looked out on the hives; the beds of flowers that spanned the distance from them to me had begun to wilt. I heard my neighbor call out from his back doorstep. "Hey, how's it going?" I must have nodded because he continued. "Hey, I needed to ask you about something."

I looked over his shoulder at his trees. I didn't know what I was going to say. The consequences seemed loose and removed from my present situation, and as he confronted me, I saw we were stuck in a Robert Frost poem.

* * *

I knew I was going to have to do something drastic. I called my brother. "I need your help," I said.

He must have either sensed the urgency in my voice or been just around the corner. He arrived in minutes with Jacob in tow. I explained the game plan, delegated responsibilities.

"So, you'll get the PVC pipe and meet me back here in a few hours?"

I went back to where I'd had the beekeeping classes and purchased a small dosage of queen bee pheromones from an instructor who—I now noticed—looked conspicuously like my brother. Given the schedule, I pressed on. We reconvened in my backyard where a small crowd had begun to gather. I looked for Tessa.

"I called everyone I could think of," Jacob said. He had put on my beekeeping suit, which was far too large for him. I imagined that among all the folds of extra material, there were spots of vulnerability.

"It's like a freak show," my brother said. "I tried to convey that with the sign."

On my way in, I had thought he captured it quite well. Then again, maybe *beard of bees* was automatically eye-catching.

I could see my neighbor watching from his back porch. He had a phone in his hand.

When I made eye contact, he gestured toward his cherry trees.

"We'd better hurry," I said, stripping down to my boxers and donning a pair of goggles. "Are you ready?" I asked my brother. He nodded. I then turned to the fifteen or so people who were gathered, most of which were students. "Are you ready?" I asked, mustering up some showmanship. Two frat boys yelled back, enraptured. Everyone else readjusted themselves in silence. I counted three cameras.

"Please, no cameras," I said, knowing it would only encourage them.

I taped the pheromones to my chest. While I was gone, my brother had found the queens. He now began grabbing at them clumsily. He put the first on my chest. I felt it crawl toward my throat. A host of other bees quickly followed and we were underway. It felt like a hot wet sleeping bag was being zipped up around me. I heard the crowd murmuring.

The first batch of stings came as my brother was adding the second hive. I felt them in my armpit. The weight of the bees on my arms had made me lower them slightly, which apparently pinched a set of bees in the region.

The only oversight in the whole process, I realized then, was that we hadn't established a safety signal—a way to bail out. I began to panic. There were still a couple hives to go at this point, and the bees were heavier now, crawling on top of each other to explore the exposed parts of my face, a million tiny fingers searching me for something they sensed but couldn't locate.

And now, they were willing to sting—to martyr themselves for a trivial cause. I felt cruel and selfish despite the pain. My lower body was going numb from lack of movement. I deserved this.

I thought I might die, and for a moment—briefly, stupidly—I was okay with that.

Somewhere in this moment, a bee found its way inside the PVC tubing through which I was breathing. I coughed. This set a chain of events in motion. The bees near my mouth and on my face were angered by this disturbance. Some stung, but remarkably, most absorbed the tremors and resumed their probing.

And then, by some miracle, I began to smell smoke. Slowly, the bees began to dissipate and my vision slowly returned. A light round of applause was breaking out, but the instigators were blurry and indistinguishable. As the heaviness lifted, I feigned an exhausted collapse, which yielded a few more stings. I didn't care. The crowd liked this and continued to clap as I lay quietly, spread eagle on the grass.

Somewhere in the distance, I could hear sirens, but I didn't care.

My brother called out somewhere above me, "He's okay, folks. Thanks for coming." I began to hear the shuffle of departing feet.

The show was over. My bees were gone, probably to the Christiansens' orchard or somewhere else more exotic. I didn't care. They had earned their freedom. I rolled over and opened my eyes. My cheeks were swollen, but nevertheless, I could see above me the stragglers curlicuing absently, separated as they were from their queen, and I felt myself reach toward them.

The sirens were closer now.

And then, from somewhere outside my field of vision, I thought I heard Tessa call out: "Bravo."

CAMP MERRY WETHER

I am fourteen when my parents send me to sheep camp. My mother drives me there in our family minivan. They have signed me up because someone at the plant recommended it. Their coworker claims it was the best summer of her son's life.

My parents are perpetually distracted and are therefore susceptible to all sorts of unsolicited recommendations and subliminal advertising. Our home is filled with bargain-priced kitsch that once made someone else's life a little bit easier.

When my mother finds the entrance to Camp Merry Wether and reads the sign: "We turn kids into shepherds," all she can say is "Are you ready to become a shepherd?" In two hours, she has a hair appointment in Lansing. A friend has recommended a stylist-alchemist who has promised to turn my mother's hair from straw into gold.

"I mean, I don't think my hair is straw," she says, "so I can hardly imagine what he'll do with it."

We make the turn and coast down a long driveway. Trees lean over us. We reach the main buildings. Cars clog the parking lot. Sheep loiter in a nearby field.

"Well, here we are," my mother says and drops me at registration.

* * *

Some of the parents stay until the flocks are determined. They sit on aluminum bleachers and fight to keep their children interested as hundreds of sheep parade by in front of us.

A boy named Cooper befriends me; his family adopts me. His mother shows me a stash of junk food inside a duffel bag. This, I learn, is Cooper's. It's contraband. It will be confiscated in a few hours, but for now, it is enough to bond us.

The sheep flow by, and we are forced to choose. Some of the other campers hop out into the show ring and examine teeth, haunches. I laugh, but Cooper says, "It's not a bad idea."

To our left, a woman has struck up a conversation with Cooper's mother. Her boy, we learn, is Mason. He's younger and won't talk with us. It becomes clear he is different. She talks about him as if he's not standing in front of her playing with her sundress. "If he can learn to take care of something else, maybe he'll feel empowered to take care of himself," she says.

Together, we look at Mason. His fly is undone, but we pretend not to notice. He continues playing with her dress. Mason's mother is lean and bronze. Everyone watches Mason swing the hem of his mother's dress from side to side. This is a moment of great possibility, but the camp director interrupts and asks her to help pick sheep for her son.

* * *

There are thirty campers. We each get ten sheep and a color. I am blue. I watch as the counselors spray a single dot on the rump of each of my sheep.

After they are done, I am given a moment with my sheep. I step among them. I feel as though I should say something inspiring to establish rapport, but they seem indifferent. Instead, I stroke their wool, which is coarse and dirty.

* * *

We acclimate quickly.

The camp population splits between four groups: religious zealots, disciplinary problems, children of professionals and intellectuals and second-generation ag kids. I loosely belong to the last group. My parents both grew up on farms, left the land and remember it more fondly than they should. But that's not why I'm here. And I find I don't have much in common with the professional children—the offspring of parents who, when faced with the choice of sending their children to be astronauts, botanists, or musicians, chose to send them to be shepherds. I have never been a child of opportunity.

Even so, most of us came here because our parents didn't know what else to do with us. Ronnie, though, is here on scholarship. He wrote an essay that paid his way, and as an additional bonus, he gets to take home a flock at the end of the summer. Never mind how they'll get them home. His mother drives a Taurus. They live in public housing.

Few talk to Ronnie, even fewer talk to the zealots. I try even though the zealots cloister themselves in the far cabins and reflect on their experience every night. They have requested this arrangement.

Sometimes, for fun, I ask them about the more troubling aspects of the camp. They have answers for everything.

Their ringleader is Harold. He intimidates the rest of us if only because he has an adult name. Once, at a dinner where we were deprived of silverware and given mismatched kitchen equipment instead—it was supposed to emphasize the importance of having the right tools—I tried to steal his turkey baster. I expected him to be angry, but he gave it to me with great flourish and offered me his wristwatch also.

The other zealots watched and whispered among themselves.

"I don't think time matters here," I said.

He smiled, and for a week, we were friends. Then, one day while making barbed wire sculptures in crafts, he stole my hot glue gun and I swore at him.

* * *

On the third day, Cooper's flock wanders out into the neighboring interstate during swimming. It could have been anyone's, but no one can stay without a flock. The director suggests it's a lesson, albeit a difficult one. He urges us to take our charges more seriously.

"If your flock is restless, you may not get to swim," he says to scattered groans. They send Cooper home with a complimentary wool blanket from the camp gift shop.

This happens at breakfast. Cooper sits down next to me. He says, "I knew I shouldn't have gone into the deep end."

"Don't be so hard on yourself," I say. "That's a nice blanket."

The dining room has been silent since the director's announcement. The food is on the buffet, but no one moves. "Come on," he yells. "Don't be sheepish!"

After breakfast, I find Ronnie crying in our cabin. Due to the loss of Cooper's flock, they've rescinded his reward flock.

"What was your essay about?" I ask, not knowing what else to say.

"They want to give me a blanket instead," he says.

"I know, I know," I say.

* * *

After Cooper leaves, I pay more attention to my own flock. And even though the sheep constantly underwhelm us with their intelligence, I am determined to shape them up.

My counselor, Jeb, a retired rodeo clown from Detroit, tries to discourage this. He says, "They don't like to be fussed over."

I ignore him and begin taking them on walks in my free time. I herd them down the lane, past the last, "They poop it, you scoop it" sign. I employ Pepper, the camp border collie, to help manage the wanderers. He's well-socialized with sheep, but at the director's suggestion, I've added a goat to my flock to calm them. It helps. Pepper often gets excited and barks at empty trees.

* * *

At night, I try to keep my sheep from being involved in the camp's games, but it happens by lottery. The first night, we play rodeo, and my sheep are chosen. The camp director's children ride them into the ring, waving their cowboy hats. We laugh at this. They are little showmen. And then each cabin chooses a cowboy to go into the ring to round up sheep. My cabin chooses me. For legal reasons, we must wear old football helmets and shoulder pads. We look like third-string kickers.

The director calls, "Ready, set, wrangle," and we charge into the ring. Behind me, my cabin chants, "We are. Mont-a-dale." It's our cabin name, but I imagine it's a prep school.

I circle my sheep. They look more confused than scared, and somehow, they let me round them up. I remain calm and chase them toward the corral well ahead of the others.

Around the campfire that night, I am a hero until the director tells us the night's game was a lesson in a sheep's personal space, something he calls "the flight zone." I was good at the game, but he tells us what we did tonight is something we should avoid in the future.

"What about your children riding the sheep?" I ask.

"Clearly that's different," he says.

A few nights later, we play "Plunder!" a modification of capture the flag where we sneak through the night and steal from the other's team's flock. We are wolves. We are barbarians. We wear dark clothes and paint our faces with mud.

The game seems vaguely paramilitary, which wouldn't be strange except the camp is not without enemies. The summer home of the Association of Leftist & Friendly Adolescents for the Liberation of Farm Animals—ALFALFA for short—has their camp on the far side of our lake. We have heard they sometimes sneak over during the night, but we are soon taught to keep vigilant watch. And we erect electric fences to keep them away.

In order to keep the sheep away from the electric fence, we take them on a field trip to the fence immediately after they are shorn. "When their coats are full," the counselors tell us, "they don't feel a thing."

* * *

I call my parents after a week.

"Do you have a girlfriend yet?" my mother asks.

"Mom."

"It's all right. You don't have to tell your mother."

"Are you coming for the final show?" I ask. It's five weeks away.

"Sure, sure."

In the background, I hear the TV. She laughs.

"What's so funny?"

"Nothing, honey. Let me get your father."

Later, when I get back home, I'll discover their new addiction is a show called *Sunday Circular*, a locally produced cable show during which a panel of experts guides you through the mountain of ads in the weekend paper and discourses on instant rebates and clearance sales.

But today, in the void of time when the phone rests on the kitchen table, I don't know what to imagine.

My father finally comes on. He says, "Hey, bud. What's new?"

I tell him I have a girlfriend.

"Well, that's great," he says. "Just don't take any of it too seriously."

"I won't," I say, "I promise."

* * *

Of course, I don't have a girlfriend. There are only two girls at the camp: Theresa and Pam. Cruelly, they become Mary and Fat Mary. And we don't have much to do with them. My parents don't know this.

They come to anatomy with our cabin in the mornings. It sometimes feels like a reprise of sex education. We learn about breeding, about how to maintain the virility of rams by shaving the scrotum and fertility of ewes by keeping them from clover. The vocabulary for much of this is spectacularly vulgar, but we don't giggle. The camp secretary, Jean, runs the class like a busy restaurant. She carries a staff and jabs the animals to point out everything from sexual organs to mutton cuts. The sheep take it. We take it too, filling out quizzes when they are pressed before it.

One day, after we've been discussing nomenclature, Thomas, one of the professional kids, raises his hand and asks, "Did you hear the one about the ewe that called off work?"

When everyone is silent, he continues. "She told her boss she was feeling under the wether."

Jean is silent. Everyone is silent. And while I feel bad for Thomas, I can't bring myself to say anything to rescue him.

* * *

The camp itself has been through several incarnations. Originally it was a cattle ranch, but somewhere in the '40s Quakers bought it and turned it into a summer camp. We still use their cabins and sometimes find their modest graffiti high on the rafters, "Derrick loves Jesus" and "God was here."

Camp Merry Wether is founded after the area's Quakers stop having kids. The director arrives and establishes an endowment for a summer camp that will teach men how to become shepherds. The Quakers misunderstand his intent, believing it to be analogy. They sell. Flocks are purchased and Camp Merry Wether is christened.

The chapel becomes a game room, but its walls are lined with large "Shepherd of the Summer" portraits. Sometimes late in the evening, I play foosball and study them. Most of the pictures are of robust farm boys who kneel beside sheep and hold ribbons, except for Mr. 1993. He looks nothing like the others. He holds a staff and crosses his arms. He looks off camera and smiles down toward the exalting masses. Some days, while the others run after the ping pong and foosballs again and again, I stare at the photo. I admire his staff and imagine he carved it in crafts. I look to his benevolent smile and wonder what strange and heroic challenges he proved himself equal to.

* * *

Starting midsummer, we all take our sheep to pasture on Fridays. We camp out all weekend.

The first time, we are all nerves and adrenaline. The world is big, and they've spent the week reiterating its dangers. We have asked questions, but it's not enough.

I ask, "What does a wild cherry leaf look like?"

Thomas asks, "Why can't we leave the sheep here?"

Fat Mary asks, "Do sheep really eat litter?"

Harold asks, "Will you all watch my other sheep if one of mine runs away?"

"You'll have your questions answered soon enough," the counselors say.

The pasture proves to be a smorgasbord of activity. This is where the counselors cut loose. They tell us to let our sheep run freely and we do. We set up camp on the hill and practice the laissez-faire method of shepherding. We watch as they carpet the neighboring hill and pick through the grass, their color dots barely visible.

Officially, we are off the camp property. The counselors decommission themselves. They send out for energy drinks and processed sugars. They leave the sheep in our care. We play cards. We place bets. We use our staffs for a game of impromptu golf. When someone returns with supplies, we have a milk drinking contest that Mary wins.

We don't have harps or poetry, but there is plenty to do.

Mason, meanwhile, has found a field guide to edible plants, and even though he sometimes ignores his sheep, he can tell the difference between wild leek and marjoram.

Ronnie climbs a tree and trains a pair of binoculars on the far side of the lake. "It's reconnaissance," he says. "We need to know where the danger will come from."

But we don't know. During the night, there is a commotion and the sheep start. We find them on the other side of a nearby ravine, but several are missing. The counselors cross-examine the night guards and determine they were passed out in a sugar coma.

I lose one sheep. Ronnie loses two. Thomas clings to five, what they've told us in the minimum for the sheep to demonstrate flocking behavior. Harold and his followers have lost one each.

Mason somehow keeps his original ten.

"This is terrible," Jeb says. Thomas is one of his favorite campers.

The zealots have already gone in search of their sheep but will return tomorrow, empty-handed.

* * *

Back at camp, activities are suspended. The director gathers us in the game room and gives us a lecture about responsibility. He points to the pictures on the wall. "Being a good shepherd is about a lot more than popularity," he says. I follow his gaze and imagine he is saying something about Mr. 1993. "It's about cunning and fortitude and the ability to remain conscious through long hours of incredible boredom."

He paces the front of the room.

"And this isn't school. Nine out of ten is not a good score. It's failure."

We all look down at our boots. We have come straight in from the pasture, and it is clear someone has stepped in something.

"Counselors," he says. "Do you have anything to add?"

Somehow, they have escaped blame. After all, they are not the shepherds. They were never given colors.

"Tomorrow, we're bringing in a set of bottle lambs. Starting with Montadale, each cabin will take turns bottle feeding them every four hours."

Then he adds, "Don't screw this up."

* * *

For the next two weeks, we work to feed the bottle lambs. At first, some of the guys find them cute, but we soon discover otherwise. They smell like overripe fruit and constantly soil themselves. And although we know their long tails are natural, we are relieved when the counselors wrap them with rubber bands and they fall off.

I volunteer for night shift. The others pawn their responsibilities off on the Marys, so I'm stuck working with them in the middle of the night. Neither are attractive creatures, but under the heat of the lamps, conversation becomes inevitable. I relearn their names. Mary becomes Theresa from Kalamazoo; Fat Mary becomes New Zealand Pam. New Zealand Pam says, "Back home, the sheep outnumber the people twenty to one."

Together, we mix the formula for the lambs. Together we gag at the smell. Together we recognize the cups in the dining hall match the ones that come in the formula.

The lambs, meanwhile, mass together in the corner of the pen, terrified. We pry them out one by one and give them the bottle. New Zealand Pam begins singing. No one says anything, but I think even the sheep must recognize its beauty.

* * *

With two weeks left, I call my parents again. I catch them on their way out of the house.

"We're going to see your grandparents tonight," my dad says.

"Great," I say. "Are you coming to the final show?"

"Of course, champ."

"I think I might win shepherd of the summer."

"Great. Anything else?" he says.

"Is Mom around?"

"No, she's already in the car, but I'll tell her you called."

* * *

The sheep continue disappearing. Except for Mason, we all lose at least one more. Thomas loses two more, and he is sent home. Surprisingly, I miss him. I approach Harold to help me organize a search party, but the night before we are to set off, he has a dream in which he finds the missing sheep reclining with bears and lions in a paradise of green. It sounds like the sort of Eden I remember seeing on the front of a Jehovah's Witness brochure during my parents' religion phase, a time when they deregulated the subject and heard offers and recommendations from people at the gym. One of the personal trainers, it turned out, was a Witness, and he came over for dinner several nights, leaving tracts on the furniture like breadcrumbs.

I tell Harold about this.

"But I'm not a Witness," he says. "Sometimes the Lord speaks to me."

And despite my protests, the expedition is canceled.

* * *

We go to pasture again a week before the show. We are more careful now. We pitch our tents among the sheep and keep alert for the sounds of distress. We are prepared for invaders. We expect disaster.

During the night, we awake to find New Zealand Pam and Theresa from Kalamazoo are gone. We struggle to understand. They have left their bedrolls and supplies, but there are no signs of struggle or notes explaining their departure.

We search the area before returning to camp. The director has little to say about our most recent mishap. He has stopped shaving and now carries a tennis racket instead of a staff.

"There are some who are not strong enough for the challenges of shepherding," he says. "And today we have seen that." He reads this like a prepared statement.

The counselors nod. They are tired. In the bathhouse, I overhear some of them talking about the magic one-week window.

Without the girls, the camp seems to disintegrate. We all lose more sheep. We grow apathetic. It has become clear that either Mason or I will be crowned "shepherd of the summer." But all I can think of is New Zealand Pam's singing.

* * *

During my final phone call home, my parents sound tired, but they assure me they're still coming.

"How do we get there?" my mother asks.

"Mom, you brought me here."

"I know that, but I'm choosing to wash the day from memory in light of that day's hair appointment."

"Uncle Jimmy's into selective amnesia now," my dad says.

My mother says, "It's not a myth."

I sigh. I tell her to look the directions up.

"Something wrong?" my dad asks.

"No, everything's as it should be," I say. "Shipshape."

* * *

The day of the show, I wake up early and go for a walk. The sky glows grayish white. The sheep are still penned in the paddock in anticipation of the show. I walk toward the game room for another look at the shepherd of the summer portraits, but there's a new lock and bolt on the door. It hasn't been there all summer.

I walk down to the lake. The morning mist billows off it like smoke. I sit on one of the overturned rowboats we stopped using after water samples were returned from a state lab. I look across the lake to where I know the ALFALFA camp must be, and I try to imagine New Zealand Pam and Theresa from Kalamazoo relaxing in an Eden on the other side of the lake. But I can't.

And so I return to the cabin. Mason is already up doing his morning calisthenics. He looks decidedly fitter than when he arrived.

I say, "I need your help with something."

He doesn't question me. He follows me to where the sheep are. Even though the show is to begin in an hour, no one is around.

"This is the last day of camp," I say.

He nods.

I ask, "Do you know how to pick a lock?"

He nods. "I just learned the other day."

While he works, I climb over the fence and step out among the remaining sheep. They are restless and agitated, so I sing, "Bo, Bo, Black Sheep."

They calm. They seem larger and dumber than yesterday, more desperate for leadership. I call out to Mason. I think about asking Mason why none of his sheep have run away, but it seems unprofessional. Instead, I ask, "How much longer?"

In response, he flips open the latch.

* * *

The parents are arriving as we lead the sheep up the driveway. Our sheep force their cars off the road and onto the grassy shoulders. Our sheep flow around the cars like water. The parents sit in confused silence, as though they've made a wrong turn and wound up in some other future at some different sheep camp.

Mason cajoles the stragglers. He's good at it and calls the sheep by name—something I'd never considered. Meanwhile, I lead. Behind me, the bottle lambs fall over themselves in an effort to keep the pace.

My parents are parked under the "They poop it, you scoop it" sign. I don't catch their attention, and for a moment, I slow our pace. They look up eventually, but at Mason rather than me. Halfway down the lane and we are near the director's house. Again, I slow my pace. I realize I am looking for someone to stop me, to say this can't be, to judge the rightness of this action. But no one does, and so Mason and I drive on, and when we reach the end of the lane, I stop and force the sheep onward into a world far wider than they can imagine.

ACKNOWLEDGMENTS

I am deeply grateful to everyone at Cornerstone Press for their work in making this book a beautiful reality: Dr. Ross Tangedal, Ellie Atkinson, Eva Nielson, Sophie McPherson, Natalie Reiter, Ava Willett, and everyone else who has spent time with these pages.

This book would not have been possible without the encouragement of the journals who published earlier versions of these stories:

"King Karate" in *Emrys Journal*

"Mars Renaissance: Eight Things a Man Should Know How to Do" with *New Limestone Review*

"Cakewalk" with *Puerto del Sol*

"Knuckles" in *Beloit Fiction Journal*

"Dutch Treat" in *Natural Bridge*

"Land of Opportunity" in *Willow Springs*

"Camp Merry Wether" with *Quarterly West*

"Trivial" in *Story*

I have been taught, inspired, and influenced by a great many writers, including classmates, colleagues, students, and teachers. This manuscript owes a particular debt of gratitude to Wendy Brenner, whose influence on my writing, teaching, and personal philosophies has been nothing short of life-changing, and to the late Philip Gerard, whose voice will forever echo in my head. I am also grateful to Thisbe Nissen for her continuing warmth and enthusiasm, and to Dan Hoyt, for taking me seriously the first time I left the house. There's no way to pay you all back, but on my best days, I'd like to think I'm passing it on.

I'm so thankful for my friends and family—too numerous to name without egregious omissions. If you've received a postcard from me over the past decade or so, please understand what small tokens these are of how much I value your humor, intellect, and generosity. And, if you've never received one, let's be in touch.

To the people who raised me: thank you. To the people I'm trying to raise: thank you. To Kara: your love and partnership has meant the world to me. I can think of a thousand times when I wasn't sure this would ever happen, and you were there for all of them.

Tim Conrad holds an MFA in creative writing from the University of North Carolina Wilmington and a PhD from Western Michigan University. His work has been published in journals such as *Story, Willow Springs, Hayden's Ferry Review,* and *Quarterly West.* He teaches creative writing at Michigan State University.